One Promise

Lynne Norris

Yellow Rose Books

Nederland, Texas

ISBN 978-1-932300-92-5
1-932300-92-9

First Printing 2007

9 8 7 6 5 4 3 2 1

Cover design by Donna Pawlowski

Published by:

Regal Crest Enterprises, LLC
4700 Highway 365, Suite A, PMB 210
Port Arthur, Texas 77642

Find us on the World Wide Web at
http://www.regalcrest.biz

Printed in the United States of America

Acknowledgements:

Writing is a solitary endeavor, publishing a book is not. I'd like to thank Anita, Donna, and Lydia for reading and commenting on the manuscript.

Thanks to the great team at Regal Crest Enterprises, especially Sue and Nann, for the time and energy they invested in the editing process and for answering all my questions.

Finally to Catherine, thank you for your patient support while I spent countless hours over the past three years writing this story.

To Catherine and Zachary, all my love.

Courage is the price that life exacts for granting peace.

~Amelia Earhart

Chapter One

RECURRENT THOUGHTS TUMBLED through Teresa Parker's mind: a promise, a tragic accident, an orphaned child. But she pushed the scenes away and leaned against the railing on the back porch of her house. The eastern sky began to brighten as the first light of dawn appeared in shades of gray over the horizon. Wisps of steam trailed up from the hot mug of freshly brewed coffee that sat untouched beside her on the rail.

Birds flitted about in the branches of the swamp maples overhanging the briskly running creek that meandered through the back of her property. A week's worth of rain had filled the stream at a time of year when it would normally be dry. A large deer stood at the water's edge; its tail flicked nervously before it ducked its regal head and drank the cold water.

Teresa lifted the mug to her lips and carefully sipped the hot beverage. She tasted the brew and closed her eyes briefly, enjoying the peaceful solitude she came to look forward to at the beginning of each day.

The days just seemed to blend together in a blur of activity. They started with getting Brian ready for school, then working long hours on the latest construction project that demanded her attention, helping with assignments sent home from school, and taking care of the regular household chores before collapsing into bed exhausted each night.

Her hectic schedule left little time for her to consider her personal life. Last night, as she put away laundry, she got lost for a brief moment staring at an old picture she found lying in the bottom of a drawer.

The picture was one of Brian's christening. Someone had taken it in the church when Teresa was holding Brian and was standing between his parents—her brother, David, and his wife, Fran. Everyone was smiling and blissfully unaware of what fate held in store for them.

Again the memory brought home, with devastating clarity,

how much her and Brian's lives had changed over the past two years.

Teresa headed into the house after a few more minutes of quiet reflection. She turned on the faucet inside the shower. The pipes groaned briefly in protest and then spit out a steady stream of hot water. She stripped off her sweats and stepped beneath the running water. She let it pound on her shoulders to lessen the ache in her muscles that she woke with each morning.

After showering quickly, she towel-dried her short, dark-brown hair. At one point, she had worn it much longer, but for practical purposes she preferred the wash and wear style better these days.

She dressed in shorts, a T-shirt, and well-worn work boots and then walked down the short hallway to Brian's room.

Opening the door, she poked her head into the room. His body was curled up under the blanket, only the top of his head visible. She walked over and shook him gently.

"Brian, it's time to wake up."

He stretched and yawned, before answering. "Mornings start too early."

"I know, but it's time to get up."

He grumbled his dissent and rolled over. "Do I have to?"

A hint of a smile twitched at the corner of her lips. "It's a school day, so yes, you have to. Do you want cereal for breakfast?"

He slowly sat over the side of the bed and eyed the clothes he had chosen the night before with Teresa's help.

"Cheerios."

"Okay. Don't take long to get dressed."

When Brian walked into the kitchen ten minutes later carrying his sneakers, Teresa had finished another cup of coffee and set out two bowls and a box of cereal for them. She watched as Brian filled his bowl and then poured in the milk. The simple motions were a stark reminder of his father.

At six, Brian was the spitting image of Teresa's brother, David. He had wavy dark hair, thick eyebrows, angular cheekbones, and hazel eyes that changed with his moods. The family resemblance between Teresa and Brian was unmistakable, and most people who didn't know them well assumed he was her son and she, a single mom.

Teresa remembered when David asked her to be Brian's legal guardian almost five years ago. Touched by the request, she felt honored, and of course, she accepted. She never gave the conversation with her brother another thought until three years later.

It was common for Brian to spend one weekend a month with

Teresa, so David and Fran could have some time alone. What became a running joke between Teresa and Brian brought a bittersweet smile to Teresa's face as she remembered.

"You're my favorite aunt, Aunt Teresa."

"Brian." Teresa lifted him high into the air. "I'm your only aunt."

"I know, but you're still my favorite aunt."

TERESA COULD VIVIDLY recall everything she did with Brian that particular weekend. After spending part of Saturday at a water park, she took him to a newly released movie he had been begging to see.

On Sunday, they went fishing, and Teresa remembered how excited Brian was about showing his father the large trout he caught.

That opportunity, tragically, never came.

When David and Fran were late returning, Teresa figured they hit Sunday traffic coming back from the Jersey Shore. She started to worry as the evening wore on, and there was still no word from them. After she got Brian off to bed, she made several phone calls to see if any family or friends had heard from them.

A hospital emergency room called her three hours after they were due home.

There had been a car accident. A drunk driver ran a red light at an intersection and plowed into David's car. Both David and Fran had died.

In the blink of an eye, Brian's and Teresa's lives were irreversibly changed.

Teresa's mother was overwhelmed with grief. Fran's parents had been traveling, and it took a day just to track them down, so it was up to Teresa to make the funeral arrangements and console a boy whose world had just been destroyed.

Breaking the news to Brian was one of the hardest things she had ever done in her life, and the memory still brought tears to her eyes.

After the phone call from the hospital, Teresa called her best friends and fell apart crying on the phone. Rich Adams and his wife, Betty, arrived on Teresa's front porch thirty minutes later, and the three of them hugged, cried, and talked long into the night about how to tell Brian.

In the end, Teresa went into the room where Brian was sleeping, sat on the edge of the bed, and watched him. He woke shortly after the sun brightened his room, and as soon as he saw Teresa, he asked the question she'd been dreading.

"Where are Mommy and Daddy?"

She tried not to cry, but the tears came anyway, and her heart felt like it was breaking with every word she uttered. "Brian, there was a car accident, and your mom and dad were hurt very badly."

"Where are they?" He sat up in bed and rubbed his eyes.

She held her arms out to him, and he crawled into her lap and rested his head against her chest. "The ambulance took them to a hospital. The doctors did everything they could, but they couldn't save them." She choked on the last words. "I'm so sorry, Brian. They both died."

"When are they coming back?"

Teresa hugged him tighter and kissed the top of his head. "Oh, sweetie, Mommy and Daddy aren't coming back. They're in heaven now."

Brian had simply started to cry.

FOR MONTHS AFTER the funeral, Teresa suffered through the dark dreams that filled her nights and the bitter memories that sucked her down like quicksand without warning. Every day she woke up, there was that split second between sleep and full wakefulness when her mind played tricks on her, and she believed David and Fran were still alive, and Brian was just sleeping over.

At first, a few well-intentioned friends called frequently to see if there was anything they could do, but it was like having salt thrown on an open wound. So she learned to function alone despite the grief and despair.

There were days when the depression would crash down over her, and it took a great effort just to get out of bed.

For Brian's sake, she continued going through the motions of daily life.

If all that wasn't enough, six months after the funeral, Teresa's lover ended their relationship. Despite their five years together, Erin was not about to put her life on hold to raise a child.

Devastated by the onslaught of emotional losses, Teresa buried her feelings and threw herself into working and providing Brian with a safe and loving home.

Subtly, over time, she sensed a change in how she felt. The feelings she had tried to banish from her heart became an insistent reminder of that soul-deep connectedness that human beings crave.

She wanted to share the simple things in life with someone, to feel that bond with another person. Someone to share a home-cooked meal with, someone to talk with about the ordinary matters that shaped their daily lives, and most important, someone who also had enough room in her heart to love Brian.

It wasn't too much to ask out of life, was it?

Teresa cleared her throat and forced away the well of self-pity she was allowing herself to fall into. "Don't forget, Brian, I'm working late, so Aunt Betty's bringing you to her house for dinner."

"I like going to Aunt Betty's for dinner." Brian tilted the bowl to his mouth and slurped the milk.

"I'm glad you do." She ruffled his hair affectionately. "Go brush your teeth."

Teresa cleaned up from breakfast, put the bowls into the dishwasher, and double-checked that Brian had everything he needed for school. At the front door, Teresa settled the backpack on his shoulders. When she was done, Brian reached up and Teresa gave him a hug.

"I love you, Brian." She planted a kiss on his forehead.

"I love you, too, Teresa."

Teresa walked him to the bus stop at the end of their street. Brian was too young and the walk just a little too far for Teresa to feel comfortable letting him go by himself. After the bus picked him up, she walked back home and got ready to drive her truck into town.

MADELINE GEDDES'S APARTMENT was quiet as she got ready to go to work. It was in stark contrast to the rowdy noise that surrounded her throughout the school day. While she waited for her kettle to boil, Maddy sliced cucumbers and tomatoes from the small garden she planted in the spring and tossed them with some lettuce in a plastic container for her lunch. When the kettle whistled, she poured the water into her travel mug and then gathered her tote bag full of lesson plans.

The first few weeks of the school year were exciting for her — meeting new students and enjoying their exuberant energy at seeing old friends and connecting with new ones. The eager young faces made her smile and reaffirmed her belief that she had made the right choice in becoming a teacher.

This year it was especially so, because she was new to the community and delighted with the opportunity to be starting her life over with a clean slate. For the first time since her relationship with Christine ended, she felt like she was finally emerging from the dark cloud of misery that had been hanging over her.

Their relationship had lasted nearly seven years. They met at college her senior year, lived together through the second semester, and moved into an apartment in New York City after graduation.

Maddy started teaching in a Manhattan public school, and Christine worked her way to junior partner at a prominent law firm on Park Avenue.

She still wasn't quite sure what went wrong. Maybe, it was the long hours they worked or the vastly different worlds in which they moved. All she knew was that whatever had drawn them together and made her believe that this was forever had slipped away without much fanfare.

She could have accepted that they no longer loved each other, as painful as the realization was, but learning that Christine betrayed her long before by taking a new lover was too much for Maddy to bear. The clues were all there, but Maddy still listened in shock one evening as Christine announced that she was in love with someone else and was moving out.

The confrontation disintegrated into an ugly shouting match punctuated by Maddy throwing a ring Christine had given to her across the room and screaming at her to get the hell out.

That was over a year ago.

During that time, Maddy's aunt died and left her some property in Morristown, New Jersey. Maddy considered moving there, and her older sister, Angela, encouraged her to look for a job teaching in one of the surrounding towns. It couldn't have worked out better. She went on an interview and received an offer for a teaching position at Woodland Elementary School.

She had been saving money to buy a house, but one look at the old Dutch barn on her aunt's property, and the view overlooking a small pond, and Maddy fell in love. With Angela's help, she found a reputable contractor, Rich Adams, to work with.

Together, Maddy and Rich drew up plans to build a single family home on the open lot. He gave her a reasonable estimate for the project, and a little more than a week later they signed a contract.

Maddy liked Rich at once. He was completely professional and every few days brought her up to speed on what was happening. As permits and approvals were obtained, the day finally arrived when construction began.

That was in June. Through the summer as the excavation made way for the poured concrete foundation and framing, Maddy finished decorating the upstairs apartment over the barn, so she could live in it until the new house was ready.

Now that the school year had started, she had somewhere else to focus her energy. She looked forward to the challenge of making a difference in her students' lives. She cherished the successes she shared with them because those moments tempered the times when she wasn't able to connect with a student on a level that she wanted to.

Not all the students were as receptive to learning as others, but it didn't stop her from trying.

She spent her evenings alone preparing lesson plans. Her favorite spot to visit on the weekends was Lewis Morris Park where she could hike or sit quietly at Sunrise Lake early in the day when it wasn't too crowded. When she needed to escape from the din of daily life, she would drive to Hacklebarney State Park, enjoy a day beneath the canopy of tall trees, and soak in the roar of the sun-dappled waterfalls.

As she drove to the elementary school, Maddy's thoughts turned to her class of first graders. They were a lively bunch with enthusiasm to spare. As usual, the students fell all along the continuum of where they should be academically and socially. Each and every one was special to her, but one child in particular struck a chord in her heart.

Brian Parker was a slender, quiet boy with dark, neatly groomed hair.

When the students chose their seats on the first day of school, she noticed that Brian gravitated to a desk closest to one of the windows overlooking the playground. She knew it could mean something as innocuous as the boy being a daydreamer, but Maddy also understood from her teaching experience that it could be a sign of other potential problems. That concerned her.

Brian was polite and a little shy, but what struck her most about him was the quiet air of sadness that seemed to emanate from deep within his soul. On one particular day, while she walked around the classroom as the students worked on an assignment, she saw Brian rest his head down on folded arms. Thinking he might be sick, Maddy knelt beside his desk. Tears were rolling down his face and a wet stain was growing on the sleeves of his sweatshirt.

"Brian, honey, what's wrong? Are you sick?"

He shook his head and wiped away his tears.

"Can you tell me what's making you cry?"

"I'm sad today," was the painfully honest answer.

Since he wouldn't tell her anything else, Maddy vowed to make a special effort to spend some time talking with him, so she could get to know him better.

After a week of working with all the kids on various assignments, Maddy realized that Brian was having difficulty focusing in class. Despite moving his seat away from the window and closer to the front of the class, she frequently had to remind him to focus his efforts on an activity the class was doing when it was obvious that his attention was elsewhere. She also noticed that he tended to shy away from the boisterous groups of kids at recess and often seemed lost amidst all the activity in a school day.

When she sat with him and worked one-on-one, Brian could

listen and follow directions and he could read and write with some effort. But left to his own devices, he seemed incapable of finishing even the simplest of tasks.

After watching him struggle, Maddy decided to talk to his kindergarten teacher. She found the young woman in her classroom one day after school putting together a project for her class.

Miss Kathleen looked up at Maddy when she knocked on the door. "Come on in, Maddy. How are you?"

"Good, Kathleen. How's your class coming along?"

"I have a good bunch of kids, so I'm hoping for an enjoyable year."

"I need to ask you a question about one of your students from last year who's in my class."

"Brian Parker?"

"How did you know?"

"I figured you would be coming down here at some point to talk to me about him." Kathleen opened her desk drawer, pulled out a folder, and handed it to Maddy. "Here, this will probably answer most of the questions you have."

Maddy carefully opened the cover, and her eyes scanned over the words in the newspaper article. "Dear God. Why didn't anyone tell me his parents were killed in a car accident?"

"It was more than two years ago. He had counseling after it happened. The principal here at the time felt it was in Brian's best interest to focus on what was ahead of him and not dwell on the past, so that was what we did."

Stunned, Maddy shook her head in dismay as she closed the folder and handed it back to Kathleen.

"You can keep it."

"I don't need to. I knew there was something wrong, but I had no idea it was something like this."

Maddy's heart ached when she realized the magnitude of what happened to Brian. In one devastating instant, his secure, familiar, nurturing world had been shattered.

Over the years, she had dealt with kids going through their parents' divorce, a sick parent, and even a couple of cases that involved child abuse at home. They were all tragic, but maybe because of the losses she recently suffered, Maddy found that she was deeply affected and concerned about Brian. The signs of trouble were there, and she feared Brian would fall hopelessly behind if he didn't get the help he needed. That was when she decided she needed to meet with his guardian, Teresa Parker, and discuss her concerns.

Chapter
Two

THE STACCATO THUMPING of a pneumatic nail gun echoed loudly through the woods as Teresa crouched on the roof and secured the final half-inch-thick sheet of plywood to the rafters. She stopped when she heard Rich's voice from where he was standing on the ladder.

"Teresa."

"What's up?" Teresa pulled a bandanna from her pocket and wiped the sweat from her forehead.

"I have to go over to the Wilson house on Vine Street."

"What's going on?" She lowered the pneumatic hammer down to Rich and then carefully stepped onto the ladder.

"They're having a problem with the plumbing inspection."

"Didn't Sam do the rough-in for the plumbing there?"

"Yeah. This is the second time now that he's having an issue with an inspector." Rich stepped off the scaffolding and followed her down the ladder.

"He better not piss them off too much. They'll be looking to give him a hard time."

"Sam's good at what he does, but he's a hothead and thinks he knows everything."

Teresa pulled a water bottle from the cooler she kept in the back of her pickup truck and hopped up onto the tailgate. "Hey, which guys are you using to help out with the roof?"

"Bill and Jay. Why?"

"They do a better job, that's all." She took a long drink of the cold water and swallowed. "Brian's first grade teacher owns this property."

"That's right, I forgot Madeline Geddes was his teacher this year. If I remember correctly, her aunt died and left the property as her inheritance."

Teresa glanced over her shoulder at the two-story barn house. The land backed up against a thick stand of trees that separated Spring Vale Road from Loantaka Reservation. She knew the area well, having roller-bladed and jogged through most of the bike trails in the park. "It's a beautiful piece of property with the pond sitting back there."

"I'll say." Rich opened his cooler and pulled out two sandwiches that his wife, Betty, had made early that morning before she left for work at Woodland Elementary. He handed one to Teresa. "Hey, have you got any plans for the weekend after this one coming?"

"Thanks." Teresa eyed him curiously. "Just the usual. Why?"

"Betty wants to have you and Brian over for a barbecue on that Saturday. You know she starts to go through withdrawals if she doesn't get to see that boy every couple of weeks."

Teresa let out a relieved laugh. "I thought you were going to tell me we had another job to add to the schedule."

"No, Betty will kill me if I take another job before I finish repairing the dock."

Teresa's eyes twinkled briefly as she took a sip of water. "I suppose we could make time in our schedule to come by. Brian really enjoys visiting with you two."

"Good, I'll tell her to expect the two of you then. I hear Brian is having dinner with us tonight."

"Yeah, I'll be by to pick him up around seven after I'm done meeting with the Jenkinses about their renovation project."

"We'll see you then."

TERESA MADE SEVERAL calls from her cell phone to confirm the timetable with the subcontractors who were doing the electrical and plumbing work. Next, she checked on the delivery date for the windows and the doors.

As she walked around the site, she heard the crunch of tires on the gravel driveway. She thought for a moment that it was Rich returning, until she saw the sunflower yellow Volkswagen Beetle roll to a stop in front of the barn.

She collected her tools and set them in the back of her truck. She caught movement in her peripheral vision as she closed the tailgate. Someone had just climbed out of the car and was looking in her direction.

For the first time, Teresa really looked at Madeline Geddes. She was a good-looking woman whom people certainly would notice. With her auburn, curly hair pulled back in a ponytail, her bangs lay slightly rumpled over her forehead. Beneath the bangs and thick brows, her angular face was without a trace of makeup; her features were striking with high cheekbones and dimples that materialized with the smile that graced her face. She was dressed casually in a cotton skirt and a loose-fitting flowered shirt. Even though her skin bore the healthy tan of someone who spent a fair amount of time outside, her cheeks were flushed from the late-summer heat.

She walked toward Teresa and held out her hand. "You must be Brian's aunt. I'm Madeline Geddes, Brian's teacher. But please call me Maddy."

"Hi, Maddy. I'm Teresa Parker." It struck Teresa as she shook hands that Maddy was someone she would have been too shy and quiet to talk to in elementary or high school. Maddy would have been one of the *cool* kids, and Teresa had never fit into those circles.

"It's nice to finally talk to you after all this time. I've seen you here working, but I was always running out and didn't have time for more than a brief hello." When Teresa didn't reply, Maddy said, "I suppose things are going to slow down a lot after the framing is finished."

"There'll be some downtime while we wait for deliveries and get the subcontractors in to do their work. There always is."

Teresa picked up several two-by-fours that were lying on the ground and stacked them by the foundation. A vague uneasiness crept over her when Maddy continued to stand there.

"I wish I could spend more time watching the actual construction."

"Most people wish they could blink and have it done. Everything's going according to schedule right now. You've got the windows and doors coming tomorrow."

"I like to see how everything gets put together."

"How long have you lived here?" Teresa asked, after a moment's hesitation.

"Unofficially, I was out here almost every other weekend since last January, repainting the inside of the apartment over the barn. I moved in at the end of the school year."

"That barn is a beautiful structure."

"I fell in love with it when I saw it."

"How do you like the area so far?"

"It's nice, but the lifestyle is so different compared to New York. There were eleven different languages spoken in the building I lived in, and as many different restaurants in two city blocks."

"New York? Is that where you grew up?"

"No, I moved there after college to take a job teaching."

"So, you left the big city for a small town like this."

"It was time for me to move on."

As the conversation lapsed, they both fell silent, and Teresa sensed that Maddy wasn't as relaxed as she was a moment ago. As the sun peeked out from behind a cloud, Teresa stepped beneath the shade tree where her truck was parked, and Maddy followed her.

"Teresa, I'm glad I ran into you today. I was going to send a note home with Brian, so we could set up a time to meet."

"Why? Is there a problem?" Immediately anxious, Teresa turned around to look at her.

"Well, yes. I'd like to talk to you, but if now's not a good time, we can schedule something that's convenient for you."

"No, you've got my attention. Now's as good a time as any."

"There are some things that Brian's having trouble with in school, and I'm concerned."

"Like what? His kindergarten teacher seemed to think he would do just fine adjusting to first grade."

Maddy tucked a lock of hair behind her ear before she went on. "She may have been right in her assessment of how he was doing then, but sometimes problems don't start to show themselves until the kids start first grade. First grade is a big change from kindergarten."

"I don't understand. Is it an issue with him not applying himself?"

"No, I wouldn't say that, and I don't want you to think it. Brian is a great kid and he tries hard. I think the transition into first grade is creating some new insecurities for him, and frankly, it's affecting his ability to learn." Maddy hesitated. "Teresa, it's only when I sit with him one-on-one that he can follow directions and complete a task with minimal redirection."

"But that's okay, isn't it? I mean, this is first grade we're talking about."

"When I give the students an assignment, Brian should be able to work independently. That's where his skills fall apart. He can't seem to concentrate long enough to complete a task, and he has a hard time following the directions I give to the class." Maddy continued when Teresa didn't say anything. "The other thing I've noticed is that he doesn't verbally express his feelings or his needs very well with me or his classmates."

Teresa felt a tightening in her chest as she thought about how much she helped Brian with his assignments at home. She bent down and picked up a couple of wood screws that were lying in the dirt. With a sudden pang of guilt, she realized there had been times when she thought he needed too much help, and all along maybe she really was just in denial.

She straightened up and jiggled the screws in her hand. "I'm not sure I know what to say. A psychiatrist treated him for a short time right after his parents died because he was crying a lot in preschool. The only thing the guy wanted to do was put him on medication. Brian walked around like a zombie for two months. It was terrible. I couldn't allow him to continue like that. After we got the doctor to wean him off the drugs, we stopped seeing the psychiatrist, and then we talked to a grief counselor every week for a few months. His advice was for me to spend time with Brian and not to push him too hard." Teresa looked at Maddy warily, expecting some kind of judgment for how she chose to handle things with Brian.

Instead, Maddy's eyes clouded with sympathy. "I'm truly sorry for the loss you both have suffered, Teresa."

Momentarily relieved, Teresa nodded her appreciation. "Do you think Brian's got a learning disability?"

"I don't know. I do know that the academic and social skills he's struggling with are ones he should be more comfortable with at this point in his development." Maddy tilted her head as though considering her words. "However, kids *and* adults tend to have a hard time concentrating when other things are going on in their lives that distract or upset them. Sometimes, what's happened in a person's life is so disruptive that he or she literally can't think clearly."

Teresa was silent for a moment. *You mean like his entire world collapsing around him.* "Well," she said, "I think what he's gone through by losing both his parents would certainly qualify. I'm open to suggestions. What do you recommend?"

"First, and I'm sure you already know this, kids do well when they can settle into a solid routine. It's a form of security. They know what to expect, and that helps them to get through each day more easily."

Teresa sighed and tucked the screws into her pocket. "I'll be honest. In the morning we do fine, but after school, I don't have the most consistent schedule."

"Who takes care of him for you?"

"Betty Adams does most of the time. Thank God for her and Rich. I don't know what I would do without them. Sometimes my neighbor Rose helps out."

"It's just you and Brian, then?"

"Yes. It's just the two of us."

"That certainly makes it more challenging."

"It does, but we've always managed to work things out. Maybe I can get a list of assignments from you, and I can work with Brian at home."

"That will help, but what he really needs is to be tutored, so he can catch up to the rest of his class."

"He's that far behind?"

"Everything they've learned so far builds on the rest of the year and prepares them for what they will learn next year. The time to help Brian is now, not in another month or when we're deciding whether to advance the students to second grade."

"I get it. Everything just snowballs."

"Yes, it does, and the longer this goes on the harder it's going to be for him to catch up." Her voice softened. "I think the most important thing right now is to keep it simple. Pick out some books he likes and read with him at home. No pressure, no critiquing, just practice. That will help him focus and develop his confidence and attention span."

"That doesn't seem too hard."

"It takes time and dedication. You have to do it three or four times a week. If you're agreeable, I'd like to tutor Brian after school. That will give me the opportunity to work with him on math skills and get him caught up to the rest of the class. What days are good for you?"

Teresa stared at Maddy in surprise. "You're offering to tutor him."

"I don't normally tutor, but Brian is a good kid, and I know he tries hard. After everything he's been through, he deserves some extra help." Meeting Teresa's gaze, Maddy said, with quiet sincerity. "I'd like to help, if you'll let me."

Teresa was silent as she considered the offer. It wasn't a difficult decision for her to make. Brian obviously needed help, and this was beyond what she was capable of doing herself. "It's very generous of you. Thank you. Mondays and Wednesdays will work out the best with my schedule the way it is."

"That's fine. I'm glad to be able to help."

"So…what can I pay you for tutoring him?"

Maddy folded her arms across her chest. "I honestly hadn't thought about it."

"You're offering us your time. That's valuable. Think about it and let me know," Teresa said, as she started to step away.

"Wait, I do have something in mind." Maddy reached out and touched Teresa's forearm. "Since you're already working here, would you mind helping me fix that old barn door that's rusted shut?"

Teresa glanced across the way to the barn. "The door on the left?"

"How can you tell from here?"

"I was looking at it the other day. I tend to notice things like that."

"So I gather." A ghost of a smile played at the corner of Maddy's mouth as her gaze traveled up to Teresa's face.

The appreciative smile unnerved Teresa, and she looked away

to hide the unexpected flush she felt coloring her cheeks.

Maddy cleared her throat. "So, then it's settled. I'll start with Brian next Monday."

"Yes. Thanks for talking to me about Brian."

"You're welcome. He's a good boy and I really want to help him."

AFTER TERESA LEFT, Maddy walked to her car and retrieved her bags. She gazed up at the old barn in appreciation. Its sturdy structure evoked a sense of security and tradition that tugged at her heartstrings.

At some point, her aunt had renovated the barn and made the upstairs her primary residence. The original mortised, tenoned, and pegged beams exposed in the ceiling looked rustic, with large knots and whorls of underlying grain visible throughout the large timbers. Maddy had set about decorating the upstairs apartment to her liking. It provided more than enough space for her to live in while the new house was being built.

She set her bags inside the door to the stairs that led up to her apartment. She walked across the way to the framed-out structure of the house. With the framing complete and the plywood installed, she was starting to appreciate the craftsmanship of the design. If things went according to schedule, she was going to be in her new home in a few months. Just in time for the holidays.

Maddy had been checking on the progress of the construction almost every day after work. Now that she had talked with Teresa Parker, she looked at the work differently.

She remembered her father saying that you could tell a lot about a person by the kind of work he or she did. From what she had seen, Teresa seemed well versed in all aspects of carpentry.

So far, she had been involved with every phase of the construction, from pouring the concrete for the foundation to framing the exterior and interior walls.

Every step of the way, Teresa's and the construction crew's work had been orderly and efficient. Maddy hoped Teresa would be involved with the rest of the project as well.

Today she had really got a good look at her. She had seen Teresa in passing many times over the past several months but never had the opportunity or reason to talk with her until now.

She decided that Teresa handled herself well today. She'd give her that. Some parents became defensive and argumentative almost immediately upon hearing their child was not doing well in school. Others felt it was the teacher's fault and thus not their responsibility to help with the problem.

Teresa had reacted in neither way. After the initial shock, she was concerned about Brian and seemed genuinely willing to get involved with helping him. That was a plus in Teresa's corner as far as Maddy was concerned.

Upstairs in what was to be the master bedroom, Maddy leaned against the frame of a window opening. She folded her arms across her chest and gazed out at the pond that was ablaze with the glow of the afternoon sun.

In a moment of quiet reverie, she wondered whether Teresa Parker thought anything about her beyond the conversation they had about Brian. *Probably not.* With a shake of her head, Maddy dismissed the foolish thought before she walked back down the steps.

Chapter
Three

WHEN TERESA PULLED up in front of Betty and Rich's house, they were both sitting out on the front steps with Brian between them. Brian finished off an ice cream cone as Teresa stepped out of her truck.

He bounded off the steps and ran over to her. She opened her arms and gave him a hug as he plowed into her. "Hi, Teresa."

"Hi, Brian. Did you have a good visit?"

"Yeah."

Teresa walked across to Betty and Rich. "Thanks for watching him."

"You're welcome. We have leftovers. You can stay and eat if you like," Betty said.

"No, thanks. Did everything work out with the inspection, Rich?"

"Yeah. I'll tell you about it tomorrow."

Betty rolled her eyes. "I told him he's not allowed to discuss it anymore tonight, or he'll have a heart attack."

"Just wait 'til you hear this one, T."

"Ah, ah. Rich, let it go for now," Betty said. "Besides, I'm sure Teresa wants to get home."

"Thanks for the invitation for next weekend."

Betty's face brightened. "We'll have fun. It will be our official end of the summer cookout."

"That sounds great. Call me and let me know what you want me to bring."

"I will."

"Brian, say goodbye." Teresa leaned closer and whispered in his ear. "Remember to thank Aunt Betty for dinner."

Teresa walked to the truck and climbed in. When Brian joined her, she turned the ignition, and the truck's engine rumbled to life.

"I talked to Ms. Geddes today."

"About what?"

"School. You and I need to have a serious discussion when we get home."

Brian immediately slumped in his seat and stared out the window.

Teresa drove in silence as memories of David and her growing up together came back to her in brief snapshots. She remembered the day their father left and never returned home.

He hadn't died, but in some respects, he might as well have. Whether her mother knew how to reach him was something that Teresa was never privy to. It had been a bitter source of arguments over the years, and one of the reasons her relationship with her mother was so distant.

She swallowed the lump in her throat when her mind conjured up an image of David's forlorn expression as their mother told them the news. She hated her father for having walked out on them.

Teresa knew how much David loved being a husband and a father. He wanted to do all the things with Brian that his father hadn't done with him. *God, life is so unfair sometimes.*

Teresa understood that Brian was still hurting terribly, although he seldom talked about it with her. Many times over the past two years, she would find him sitting alone by the creek with his knees tucked up underneath his chin, staring out at the water.

She would sit beside him for a while, and on a few occasions, Brian had simply curled up on his side, laid his head in her lap, and cried. It broke her heart, and Teresa wished she could take his pain away.

Teresa glanced over at Brian as she turned down the gravel road that led to their humble two-bedroom ranch home. She could tell by the restless tapping of his fingers on the door handle that he was growing more anxious with each passing minute.

She let the truck roll to a stop in the driveway and then switched off the ignition. When she turned to Brian, she was surprised to see him peering back at her cautiously from beneath his bangs.

"Are you mad at me, Aunt T?"

The seldom-used endearment made her heart ache. After his parents died, Brian had stopped calling her his aunt and just used her first name. It still caught her by surprise how even now, the simplest things, like an endearment, were affected by the loss of his parents. Teresa wrapped an arm around his shoulder and hugged him.

"I'm not mad at you, but we've got some things to work out."

"You mean about school?"

Teresa pulled away and opened the door. "Yes."

"Oh." Brian climbed out of the truck and reluctantly followed

Teresa toward the house.

She unlocked the front door and held it open for him. "I'm going to grill a couple of hotdogs. Do you want one?"

"Yes, please." Brian looked up at her briefly before he walked inside.

Thirty minutes later, with the hotdogs grilled and baked beans warmed, Teresa and Brian sat at the worn wooden table on the back porch eating.

"Why didn't you tell me you were having trouble with your schoolwork?"

Brian was silent for a moment and then said, "I didn't want you to think I was stupid."

Stricken, Teresa reached across and lifted his chin, so he was looking at her. "Brian, I don't ever want you to believe I would think that about you. You're a smart kid." She dropped her hand and continued. "Remember how we've talked about making good choices and bad choices?"

"Yes," Brian said, and then bit into his hotdog.

"This wasn't a good choice. When you're having trouble with something, I can't help you if you don't talk to me. Do you understand?"

"Yes."

"Good." They finished eating in silence as Teresa thought about everything Maddy had told her.

When he finished the last of his hotdog and roll, Brian stood up to bring his plate inside.

"Come back out here, so we can talk some more," Teresa called after him.

She rested her forehead in her hands after Brian went inside. The food eased the emptiness in her belly, but her head still ached, and she guessed it was from the conversation she had with Maddy about Brian. She scrubbed her face with her hands and then walked over to the steps where she sat down to wait.

When Brian returned, he sat on the top step beside her. "Are you going to ground me?"

"No, I'm not going to ground you. Ms. Geddes is concerned about you falling behind with your schoolwork. I want you to tell me what's been going on."

Brian lowered his head. "I don't know. I just can't do the work."

"Why? There has to be a reason."

"I don't know."

Teresa felt frustrated but reminded herself about what Maddy had told her earlier about him being distracted. Maybe he really didn't understand why he was having a hard time in school. "I wish you would have talked to me, Brian."

"It's not a big deal."

"Yes, it most certainly is."

"I'm sorry." He ducked his head, and she could see his cheeks color as they often did when he got upset.

"Ms. Geddes offered to help you with math."

"She did?"

"Yes, and I'm going to help you, too. You and I are going to spend time reading together at night."

"Can I still watch TV?"

"Not as much as you've been. This is much more important."

"Oh. But wait." Brian looked at Teresa with a concerned expression on his face. "When is Ms. Geddes going to help me?"

"I decided on Mondays and Wednesdays after school."

"That stinks." Brian stood up and jammed his hands into his pockets. "I don't want to stay after school."

"I know you don't, but you're behind, and you need the help to catch up."

"It's not fair." He stuck his lower lip out in a pout and kicked his shoe against the step.

"It's not about what's fair." Teresa reached out and gripped his arm gently. "If you fall too far behind, you'll end up having to get tutored this summer. You don't want to blow the whole summer going to school, do you?" She didn't want to tell him he could be left back.

Brian shook his head. "No."

"I didn't think so." Teresa let her hand drop to her lap. "If you had told me sooner that you were having trouble, we could have worked together. You didn't, so now we have a bigger problem to deal with. Getting you tutored is going to help get you caught up in school. Do you understand that?"

He fought back tears. "I'm sorry, Teresa."

She pulled him into a hug. "Don't be sorry. Just make sure you do the work that you have to with Ms. Geddes and me."

"I will," he promised.

AFTER HIS BATH, Teresa walked into Brian's bedroom to check on him. She pulled the sheet up over his shoulders and was surprised when he opened his eyes and looked up at her. She sat on the edge of his bed and rubbed his back as he lay quietly on his side.

If she closed her eyes, she could recollect what he looked like as a baby sleeping in his crib. It was hard to believe sometimes that he was growing up so quickly.

"Teresa?"

"What?"

Brian rolled onto his back. "Do you miss Dad?"

"I miss him everyday, sweetheart." Teresa squeezed his shoulder. "Your mom, too."

"Do you think they're in heaven?"

Teresa felt a tightening in her throat and closed her eyes briefly before she answered. "Yes, I do."

Brian's expression turned serious. "When I think about them, I can't see them like I used to."

The last words were a whisper, and Teresa wrapped her arms around Brian and held him tightly as he started to cry. She rocked him, and after a few minutes, his sobbing dropped to a whimper. Teresa's heart broke watching him suffer through his emotional roller coaster.

She settled him into the bed and ran her hand through his hair. "Brian, your mom and dad are always in your heart."

"I love you, T," he whispered.

She leaned over and kissed him on the cheek. His eyes were heavy, and they fluttered closed.

"I love you, too."

Teresa waited until his breathing fell into a deep, regular pattern before she stood up and turned off his light.

She walked outside onto the back porch and sat on the top step. Overhead, the stars were illuminating the night sky, and the moon was just rising over the treetops.

Teresa let the peacefulness surround her and concentrated on the gentle breeze that rustled the branches of the trees. As unpleasant as it had been for both of them, she was glad she had the conversation with Brian tonight. Some of the walls he had been throwing up over the past few weeks were set aside for now, and at least she had a better insight into what was going on with him.

Two years into being a parent, and there were many days when she wondered how good of a job she was doing with Brian. She had never planned to have children of her own.

IT WAS A blazing hot Saturday afternoon in August. The Jersey tomatoes were starting to come into season, and the corn was sweet and juicy. Fran was playing with Brian in the small wading pool, and Erin was inside mixing a batch of her famous margaritas. David had the charcoal grill fired up, and he and Teresa watched as the coals turned white hot.

"Fran and I have been talking about who we want to take care of Brian if something happens to us."

"I thought you guys wanted her parents to be his guardians."

"We talked about it, but we came up with more reasons why we didn't want Brian to be raised by them. Besides, last week they told us they're moving out to Arizona to live in an over-fifty-five community."

"Oh? When did they decide this?"

"I guess they always wanted to do it, and now it seems they can."

Fran came walking toward them carrying Brian in her arms. "Say 'hi, Aunt Teresa.'"

Brian gurgled something close and held his arms out to her.

"Hi, Brian." Teresa gladly accepted him and held him in her arms.

"Teresa, David and I want you to be Brian's guardian." Fran leaned in and kissed Brian's head.

Teresa looked between her brother and sister-in-law. "You guys are serious about this?"

"You don't have to give us an answer today. Take some time and think about it."

"Everything would be set up in a trust for Brian," David said.

"I–I'm honored you would ask me."

"You're my sister. What better choice is there? You raised me."

Later, when Teresa told Erin what David and Fran had asked of her, Erin simply shrugged her shoulders.

"If something happens, Teresa, that's a big responsibility to bear."

"I know, but he's my brother, and there's nothing I wouldn't do for him."

TERESA LEANED BACK against the railing and stretched her legs out. Her thoughts turned to Madeline Geddes. Even though her talk with Maddy had been mostly about Brian and school, Teresa found that she enjoyed the interaction with her.

She didn't get much opportunity to hang out and talk with other people these days. It was nice to talk with someone who was intelligent and had a sense of humor. Maddy seemed like a nice person, genuine and caring.

There were a few moments today when she got the impression that Maddy was flirting with her. Teresa sighed and closed her eyes.

Other than Maddy being Brian's teacher, Teresa didn't know very much about her. She was surprised and touched by Maddy's offer to help him. As Teresa's mind immediately conjured up an image of Maddy's full lips curved in a smile, something stirred in her belly. She would be lying if she didn't acknowledge that she was attracted to her.

There was no reason to waste time thinking about it, though. Teresa was sure the exchange earlier today was purely innocent.

Knowing how hard it had been on Brian when Erin walked out of their lives, Teresa was reluctant to test those waters again anytime soon. Brian didn't understand why someone who had been such a big part of their lives and had been his friend could just turn around and leave one day.

Teresa shook her head and buried her face in her hands. What did she possibly expect to gain, hiding behind the fact that love and life had caused her more pain than she could bear some days? She had been in a dark and lonely place emotionally for a long time.

She still had the pills the doctor had given her when she had been in a really bad way. There were pills for the anxiety and depression, and pills to help her sleep.

Awhile back, she had stopped taking them because they made her feel like a shadow of herself, numb not only to the emotional pain but also to life itself.

She felt as though she were at an impasse, unable to move on with her life. A part of her was content with that. It was safe, and there were no expectations beyond what she had been doing for the past two years.

But she also despised the part of her that didn't want to crawl out of the dark, empty hole and take an active role in life again.

Why, though, would she risk that kind of heartache again for either of them?

Her number one reason for talking with Maddy today was her brother's son. Brian was her priority, not chasing shadows of possibilities.

Chapter
Four

IT WAS SEVEN o'clock at night. Maddy was standing in her kitchen sipping a margarita and feeling pitifully grateful that it was Friday. The school day hadn't started out particularly miserable, but halfway through, Maddy wished she had stayed home in bed.

Two little boys in her class got into a scuffle at recess over who kicked the ball first during a game of kickball, and one boy bit the other. She separated them before either one got hurt badly, and she escorted them to the principal's office.

Unfortunately, that interaction set the tone for the rest of the class. Maddy had spent the first part of the afternoon reining in some unruly and rambunctious students and was grateful when the dismissal bell rang. With the school day finally behind her, she had to deal with the parents of the kickball fighters. Both were angry their kids had gotten into trouble and tried to place the blame squarely on Maddy's shoulders for not supervising the boys more closely. She felt like a referee, and judging from the parents' behavior, she understood better why the boys behaved the way they did with their peers.

Maddy was relieved to be driving home until an elderly driver ran a red light. By braking hard and swerving, she narrowly missed being broadsided by the man's four-door sedan. Thankfully, she hadn't been hurt, and her car was undamaged; but she was stunned by the narrow escape.

By the time she finally made it home, she was ready for a drink to take the edge off her agitation. It wasn't that she drank often, but she'd had enough and just wanted to relax. She took another sip of her margarita.

That was when the phone rang.

With a feeling of irritation, Maddy sighed and picked up the phone.

"Hello?"

"Maddy, it's me."

"Christine?"

One minute she'd been gradually allowing the stress of the day to ebb, and the next, the emotions that plagued her during their breakup smothered her.

"Please don't hang up on me, Maddy."

"What do you want?" Maddy rubbed the bridge of her nose, paced across the room, and sat on the couch.

"Just a chance to talk to you."

"Why now, after all this time?" She sat back and curled her legs up underneath her.

"Maddy, please. I know I've made a lot of mistakes."

"Mistakes? Christine, you cheated and lied to me about it. That's more than a mistake."

"I know and that's why I called. I'm sorry for what I did to you...to us. It was stupid and arrogant. Can you ever forgive me?"

Maddy tilted her neck back over the couch and closed her eyes. She felt a terrific headache coming on. "What difference does it make now? I've moved on with my life. You have, too."

"Because I still love you. God, I miss you."

"Christine, I don't know what you expect me to say."

"That maybe there's still something left between us. I just wanted to hear your voice. It's been hard lately. Tina broke up with me the week after she was promoted to junior partner."

"I'm sorry to hear that." A part of Maddy was sorry, but the wicked side of her was happy that Christine had got a taste of her own medicine.

"Maybe we can get together sometime over coffee and talk. You don't have to come here. I can take a train or drive out there one day."

"Chris, I really don't think that's a good idea."

"You don't have to give me an answer now. Just think about it."

"All right. I have to go. Good night."

When she hung up the phone, Maddy finished her first margarita and mixed herself a second one. She hadn't expected to hear from Christine and wasn't sure how she felt about her request.

She had spent just over six years with Christine only to be deceived and betrayed in the end. Maddy couldn't imagine what point there would be in meeting and talking with her. Why now?

Maybe what bothered her more was that she really hadn't moved forward with her life. She had allowed her work and the new house to consume her, and she pretended to the world that she was fine.

SATURDAY WAS BEAUTIFUL, with the trees just starting to show the first signs of color. Earlier in the week, Angela had called

and made a date for the two of them to go to the Hound and
Harrier Run at Loantaka Park today. The Run was an annual event
to benefit the Saint Hubert's Animal Welfare Center. Several of the
local animal shelters brought pets in the hopes of getting them
adopted, and local artists joined in by selling their works for the
charity.

The events began with a three-mile run, and Angela made sure
they were there early enough to see one hundred fifty excited dogs
and their owners at the start of the race.

"Did you go out last night?"

Maddy stooped and scratched the floppy ears of the golden
retriever puppy that had crawled under the table and pressed its
cold, wet nose against her ankle. "Oh, hello. Aren't you cute?" She
cast a cursory glance at her sister. "No, I was home."

"Really." Angela studied a hanging copper dog sculpture that
spun in the light breeze. She whispered in Maddy's ear when she
stood up. "I called and no one answered."

Maddy slowly fixed her gaze on Angela's not-so-innocent
smile. "It's not what you think. I turned the ringer off and went to
bed early."

"Why?"

Maddy sighed. "Christine called me last night."

"I hope you told her to go jump off a cliff."

"She got dumped by her girlfriend."

"Yes!" Angela made a fist and pumped her arm. "Sweet
justice."

"Tell me how you really feel, Angela."

"It serves her right. She blew a good thing when she cheated
on you." Angela rested a hand on Maddy's arm and said, "I wish
you would get out and meet some people."

"I'm not exactly into the bar scene." Maddy frowned and
stepped away from the booth as the man and woman seated in it
clearly had stopped their conversation in order to listen to theirs.

"Who said anything about a bar? One of the girls at work met
the guy she married at a bookstore. Now, there's a nice place to
meet somebody."

"So is school, for that matter."

"Really, have you met someone?" Angela gave Maddy a
hesitant smile.

"Not in the sense that you're thinking about."

Tired of the crowds milling around them, Maddy led the way
past the last cluster of booths. A few feet away, they stopped at a
vacant park bench beneath the shade of a whitewashed gazebo.
Maddy sat down and crossed her legs.

Angela sat beside her. "Maddy, I just want you to be happy."

"I know. I'm just not particularly interested in being used again anytime soon."

"Listen, I know Christine betrayed your trust, but don't let what she did keep you from falling in love again."

Maddy was starting to regret having come with Angela to the event. The last thing she wanted was a lecture on how she needed to move on with her life.

As far as she was concerned, she was moving on at her own pace. She wasn't in a rush to get involved with anyone and was more than happy to spend time alone while she got her life back in order.

She stared off at the baseball field in the distance and folded her arms. "Angie, please spare me the lecture on love and romance. When and if the right person comes along, I'll know it."

TERESA AND BRIAN skirted around most of the foot traffic from the benefit that was taking place at the park. They walked down the paved bicycle path flanked on both sides by tall trees, large ferns, and dense undergrowth. They passed by many people walking their dogs after the race, and Brian stopped to admire each one.

"Do you think we can get a dog, Teresa?" Brian asked, after spending a few moments petting a young Labrador retriever that had pulled its breathless owner across the bike path to greet him enthusiastically.

"I don't think it would be very fair to the dog," Teresa said, as they walked away. "You're at school, and I work all day. Besides, who's going to take care of it?"

"I would take care of it."

Teresa cast a sidelong glance at him. "Maybe we can talk about this after you've gotten back on track at school."

"Okay. Race you!" Brian cried out as he broke into an all-out sprint down the bicycle path toward the baseball field.

"Oh, no, you don't." Teresa shouldered her duffel bag and took off after him. She arrived at the pitcher's mound, dropped her bag filled with baseballs on the dirt, and rested her hands on her knees while she caught her breath.

Going to the park was their Saturday afternoon ritual. Sometimes, they would walk over to the pond by Kitchell Road and fish, other times like today, they played baseball.

"Are you ready?"

"Ready!" Brian tapped the end of his bat on home plate.

Teresa tossed the first ball across the plate.

"Low and inside," Brian said and banged the ground with his bat.

"Hey, don't be too picky up there."

Teresa pitched nine more balls, four of which Brian hit solidly out of the infield. They were just finished gathering up all the baseballs and were ready to start over again when someone called out to them.

"Do you need a catcher?"

Teresa pushed up the brim of the baseball cap she was wearing. "Oh, hi. I didn't expect to see you out here." She tossed the ball up into the air and casually caught it as she walked across the infield to meet Madeline Geddes.

"My sister and I came out to watch the race." Maddy pointed to where she had left Angela sitting on the bench.

"I saw you hit the last couple, Brian. They were quite good."

"Thanks, Ms. Geddes." Brian beamed with pride at the compliment. "Do you play baseball?"

Angela let out a sharp laugh as she walked up behind Maddy. "She wasn't called Mad Dog Geddes for no reason."

"Mad Dog Geddes?" Teresa raised her eyebrows. She suddenly regarded Maddy in a different light.

Maddy glared ruefully at her sister. "Thanks, Angela. Teresa this is my lovely sister, Angela. Angela, this is Teresa and her nephew, Brian, one of my students."

"Nice to meet you, Teresa and Brian." Angela shook their hands.

"So how did you rate that nickname?" Teresa asked, when they had walked a few feet ahead of Brian.

Maddy shot her a playful, laughing look. "I'll tell you another time."

"I'll hold you to it." Teresa said with a smile and walked back to the pitcher's mound. "Batter up, Brian."

After several good hits, Brian took great pleasure in smacking the ball past the infield and sprinting around the bases.

"Throw it home," Maddy called from behind the plate.

Teresa picked up the ball and threw it to Maddy. It hopped once and Brian swerved around Maddy as he stomped onto home plate and did a victory dance.

"Give me a high five." Maddy held her palm up, and Brian smacked it enthusiastically.

"Nice running, Brian," Teresa called as she walked back to the pitcher's mound. "How about giving Ms. Geddes a try up at bat?"

"Okay."

Teresa tossed the ball up in the air as she waited for Maddy to step up to the plate.

"Are you ready?"

"Whenever you are."

Maddy settled into a relaxed stance and waited for the pitch. She swung hard and launched the ball out of the infield.

"Whoa..." Brian shouted as he watched the ball fly over his head.

They played for a few more minutes before Angela walked over behind home plate.

"Maddy, we have to leave. Tom's taking me out tonight, and I have to run some errands this afternoon."

"That was a lot of fun," Maddy told Brian as she handed him a ball.

"Can we do this again next weekend?" Brian asked as he walked alongside Teresa.

"Brian, I'm sure Ms. Geddes is busy just like we are on the weekends."

Brian's frown softened when he heard the chimes coming from an ice cream truck. "Ooh, ooh." He danced around. "Teresa, can I have some ice cream? Please."

"Yes." She stopped walking and dug in her pocket for some money. "Here." She handed a couple of dollars to Brian, and he took off running.

"Thanks, T!" he called over his shoulder.

A grin graced Maddy's features. "It was nice to spend some time with Brian before I start tutoring him on Monday. We broke the ice a little today, I think."

"You sure did." Teresa felt very at ease as she walked beside Maddy. "I don't think Brian ever considered that his first grade teacher could hit the ball as far as you did today."

"Hey, Maddy, I have to get going," Angela called impatiently from where she was standing in the parking lot.

"I'll be right there." Maddy stopped as if uncertain of what to do next. "It was nice to see you, Teresa."

"You, too, Maddy." Teresa was surprised to feel an unexpected twinge of regret that Maddy was leaving.

ANGELA WAS WAITING with her arms resting on the roof of her car as Maddy approached. "So, is that the *someone* at school?"

Maddy stopped with her hand on the door and cast a fleeting look back at Teresa. "Maybe. I don't know."

Angela watched Teresa walk to the opposite end of the parking lot. "She seemed happy to see you." Maddy cast her eyes skyward, and Angela laughed. "Things might get interesting for you after all."

"I'm tutoring her nephew. That's all."

"Mmm, what gives with that?"

"His parents died in a car accident two years ago."

"That's terrible." Angela tapped her fingers on the roof of her car. "Explains the sad eyes on both of them though."

"It's bad enough to lose one parent, but both...God, life is just not fair sometimes."

"Lord, Maddy, you sure know how to pick'em."

"What are you talking about?"

"You know what I'm talking about. Get in the car." Angela shook her head in amusement as her sister climbed in.

Chapter
Five

BRIAN WALKED OUTSIDE Monday afternoon after the bell rang to dismiss school. Amidst the commotion of all the children leaving, he walked quietly alongside his friend Steven.

"Hey," Steven said, "my mom isn't here yet. Let's go play on the playground."

"I don't know. I'm supposed to wait for Ms. Geddes."

"Come on, Brian. I'll race you to the slide."

Brian glanced back at where the teachers, including Ms. Geddes, were watching the students and decided he had a few minutes yet to play. "Last one there's a rotten egg."

They raced up the hill to the playground. Brian beat Steven and scrambled up the slide ahead of him. He grabbed the bar at the top, swung his legs out, and landed on the slide with a resounding thump. He slid down to the bottom and ran back around just as Steven made it to the bottom and jumped to his feet. This went on for a couple of minutes.

"Brian!" He spotted Ms. Geddes walking toward him from the parking lot.

"Brian, it's time for us to go in. Steven, your mom's waiting for you."

"Okay. See you tomorrow, Brian." Steven took one last run on the slide and sprinted down the hill.

"Let's go inside and get started, Brian."

With a forlorn expression on his face, Brian stayed rooted in place watching as Steven left with his mother.

"Brian?"

"Mom used to pick me up after school."

"I'm so sorry, Brian..."

"My dad's car was hit, and they...they both went to heaven." Brian swallowed the lump he felt forming in his throat and fought back tears. He wasn't sure why, but he was glad that he shared with Ms. Geddes what happened to his parents.

Maddy looked at Brian for a long moment before she spoke

again. "I can't imagine how you must feel."

"Can we go inside now? I'm thirsty."

Maddy briefly laid a hand on his shoulder. "I bet if you ask one of the ladies in the cafeteria, she'll give you something to drink."

Together they walked across the parking lot and into the school building.

"What are we going to do?"

"Don't worry. I've got a game I think you'll like to play."

"What kind of game?" He looked up at Maddy suspiciously.

"It's called Junior Monopoly."

"I've never played Monopoly before."

"I think you'll enjoy it once you learn the rules."

They stopped by the cafeteria first. All the chairs were set up on the tables with their legs in the air, and one of the janitors was mopping the floor.

"Hi, Mrs. Wilson," Brian said to the rosy-cheeked, dark-haired woman behind the counter.

"Hello, Brian. What are you doing here late today?"

"Getting some help."

"Well, we all need help sometimes. Don't we, Ms. Geddes?"

"Yes, we do."

"What can I get for you, Brian?"

Brian dug in his pocket, pulled out three quarters, and set them on the counter. "Can I get a chocolate milk?"

"Of course, you can, sweetie." She retrieved the milk from the refrigerator and handed it across to him. "This one's on me, Brian. Keep the change for next time."

"Thanks."

"Anything for you, Ms. Geddes?"

"No, thank you."

When they got to the classroom, Brian eagerly took the game that Maddy handed to him and removed the lid from the box. When he realized that Maddy expected him to give out the money and read the cards for the game, Brian felt his face flush.

It turned out all right, though, because Maddy helped him when he was stuck, mostly by asking questions that helped him to figure out what he needed to do.

As Brian rolled the dice, counted out the spaces, and picked up his first card to read aloud, Teresa, on the other side of town, was standing on a ladder that leaned against the second story of Maddy's house.

TERESA NEVER PARTICULARLY minded heights, and it was at least ten degrees cooler outside than inside the house, so she was glad to be doing this part of the window installation.

"Last one. Here it comes, T." Rich carefully maneuvered the window casing through the framed opening.

It took a fair amount of effort, but Teresa was able to pull the window into place. As Rich pushed the frame from the inside, Teresa used her power drill to start securing the flanges in place against the exterior sheathing.

She was almost finished when she heard the rumble of a car engine approaching on the gravel road that led onto Maddy's property.

Teresa checked the position of the window with her level before she drove the remaining screws in place.

Rich slid the window open and stuck his head out. "That better not be the building inspector."

Teresa glanced over her shoulder. "I can't tell from here."

At that point, a sporty black BMW parked a fair distance away from both trucks. It wasn't until Teresa saw a tall, blonde woman step out of the car that she paid her any mind.

The woman removed her sunglasses and tossed them into the car. She ran her fingers through her hair and ruffled her bangs before checking her reflection in the side mirror of her car. Finally, she straightened her T-shirt while she glanced around the property and then walked across the yard to the house.

"That," Teresa said, "is not the building inspector."

"No, but she sure looks like trouble." Rich ducked back inside the window.

Teresa leaned in to talk to him. "Why do you say that? Do you know her?"

"No, but Betty ran into her at the school not long after Maddy moved here. Said she was asking questions about Maddy but didn't want to leave her name or any kind of a message. "

Teresa clucked her tongue. "I wonder what that's about?"

"Don't know and I don't want to know. I'm going to get the tools together. That's all we can do for today."

Teresa unplugged her drill and let the extension cord snake through her hands. A small puff of dust exploded off the ground when the plug struck the dirt.

The woman stopped at the base of the ladder, shielded her eyes with a well-manicured hand, and looked up at Teresa.

"Excuse me. I'm an old friend of Madeline Geddes, the woman who lives here."

Teresa felt a completely unexpected surge of jealousy. "There's nobody home right now."

"Do you have any idea what time she might be back?"

Teresa wasn't sure what irritated her more, the question or the cool way this woman looked at her when she asked it. Still standing up on the ladder, Teresa paused and took her time looking around at the yard before she settled on an answer.

"No, I don't know what time the owners usually come home."

"Owners?"

Teresa heard the slight rise in the woman's voice and felt a sense of satisfaction as she climbed down the ladder. At the bottom, she picked up a cable and carefully coiled it.

Teresa knew Maddy was at school tutoring Brian until four o'clock, but she had absolutely no intention of sharing any of that information with the blonde.

"Excuse me. Did you say owners?"

"I'm sorry, what did you say your name was?" Looking at this self-possessed young woman, Teresa wondered what connection she had with Maddy's past.

"Christine Stewart."

"Why don't you leave her a note or call and leave a message." Teresa didn't wait for an answer as she noisily lowered the extension ladder.

She pointedly ignored the woman as she carried the ladder to Rich's truck.

"Here, let me take that," Rich said.

"You were right." Teresa helped him lift the ladder up onto the roof of the truck.

"About what?"

"Her asking questions about Maddy." Teresa motioned her head toward where she had left the blonde standing in a huff.

"Betty didn't like her one bit."

"I bet she didn't. I'll see you tomorrow, Rich."

"You're leaving me here alone with her?"

"I'm sure you can handle her," Teresa said, with a smile. "I've got to pick up Brian."

"Paybacks, Teresa. Just remember."

"Yeah, yeah." Teresa waved a hand at him as she walked toward her truck.

She knew Rich would handle the rest of the equipment and tools, and she didn't want to be late picking Brian up from school. That was when she remembered her agreement to help Maddy fix the barn door.

She could see part of the problem as she neared the barn. The hinge side of the door was warped. It needed to be shaved down to get it to sit right against the frame. The hinges themselves were badly rusted, but nothing that a wire brush, a sander, and some oil couldn't take care of.

As Teresa drove to the school, she felt badly for her rude

behavior toward Maddy's friend, but something about the woman just twisted her insides into a knot.

She wondered, as she mulled over the first conversation she had with Maddy, if Christine was an old lover trying to get back into Maddy's good graces. Teresa fervently hoped that wasn't true. She was attracted to Maddy, and she had the feeling from their meeting on Sunday that Maddy was attracted to her as well.

Teresa snorted, disgusted with herself for thinking that way, but she couldn't keep her mind from wondering about Maddy.

When Teresa got to the school, Brian was already standing outside with his backpack slung over one shoulder. As soon as she stepped out of her pickup truck, he leapt off the steps and came running. Maddy walked behind him smiling.

"Hi, Aunt T." He gave her a one armed hug. "Do you have any food? I'm starved."

Teresa inclined her head toward the back of the truck. "In the cooler. How'd your tutoring go?"

"We played Monopoly."

"Monopoly?" Teresa watched Brian run past her to the truck.

"Actually, it was Junior Monopoly," Maddy said when she got closer to Teresa. "We used it to work on reading and some math skills."

"Sounds like fun." Teresa turned toward the truck to see Brian meandering around the empty lot. "Brian, wait for me by the truck while I talk to Ms. Geddes, please."

"Okay," he said, around a mouthful of roast beef sandwich.

"How did he do?" Teresa asked as she walked with Maddy.

"He did well with word recognition. He knows how to read more words than he thinks he does. I made him do the math, like counting nickels, dimes, and pennies when we bought properties. When he was stuck, we worked it out on the blackboard together. He gets frustrated easily, but with a little help, he can figure out what he needs to do."

"I would never have thought of using a game to teach reading and math."

"It's a good way to make him apply the skills that we've covered in class and not just regurgitate the material." Maddy looked over at the truck, smiling. Brian had made short work of the sandwich. "Is he always that hungry?"

Teresa gave a quick laugh. "When he's a teenager, I'm going to need a second job just to pay the food bill in our house."

Maddy glanced back at Teresa and her expression turned somber. "He talked a little about losing his mom and dad."

"He must feel very comfortable with you to have said anything." Teresa shifted her weight and tucked her hands into her pockets. "He's a strong little boy, but I worry about him."

"You've helped him hold it together these past two years. That's a reflection of you, Teresa."

Teresa felt a warm flush in her cheeks. She looked down at the ground before smiling back at Maddy.

"Thanks."

"You're welcome."

"I looked at the barn door today. It shouldn't be too difficult to fix. Let me know when you want to take care of it, or else I could just fix it myself during the week."

"No, no." Maddy waved a hand emphatically. "If I'm going to be a homeowner, I want to start learning how to do some of these things."

"Well, Brian is spending part of the day with a couple of friends on Saturday. How does 10 o'clock sound?"

"Perfect." Maddy reached up and tucked a wayward strand of hair behind her ear.

"I'll see you then." Teresa backed away, then, stopped. She wasn't sure whether she should tell Maddy about the woman who came to her house, but as Teresa looked at her standing there, she decided it would be better if she did. "Maddy."

"Yes?"

"A woman stopped by your place this afternoon. She was asking for you."

Maddy's eyes widened. "Did she give her name?"

"Christine Stewart." Teresa had her answer by the expression on Maddy's face. "I told her I didn't know what time the owners usually came home."

The smile she got in return was priceless, and as she walked back to her truck, she was sure she had made the right decision.

Chapter
Six

TERESA LOOKED FORWARD to seeing Maddy on Saturday with a mixture of nervousness and eagerness that she hadn't experienced since high school. She thought of Maddy on several occasions over the next couple of days.

It was ridiculous. She hardly knew the woman, and here she was feeling like an adolescent with her first crush. As she lay in bed Friday night, she could picture Maddy the first day she met her, dressed in that long flowing skirt and loose fitting blouse that left much to her imagination. Even though she didn't know Maddy well, she sensed an inexplicable undercurrent between them each time they talked.

Every time she closed her eyes, she saw Maddy's face, her lithe body, and quirky smile.

Of its own accord, one of her hands moved up over her pajama top and caressed her breasts. Teresa's breathing quickened, and she felt her nipples harden in response to the touch of her hand.

How long had it been since she felt aroused like this?

She moved her other hand lower and slipped it beneath the waistband of her pajamas. Her fingers grazed over the curls of hair before sliding lower. She was surprised to feel the slick moisture covering her inner lips, and she gasped as she rubbed her fingers over her clitoris.

"Oh, Maddy," she whispered without hesitation.

Her body responded quickly to the fantasy she created in her mind. Oh, dear God, she could imagine the softness, the sweetness of Maddy's mouth on hers. As Teresa touched herself, she envisioned Maddy teasing her nipples while her tongue stroked and tasted her body. It took several fervent strokes before she reached a deep, shuddering climax that covered her fingers in her own fluid. Teresa bit down on her lip to keep from crying out. It was over too fast, and she was left feeling empty and wanting.

She found it difficult to relax as Maddy's face drifted in and out of her dreams. Teresa tossed and turned for what seemed like hours before she finally dozed off in a fitful sleep.

It was no surprise that she overslept on Saturday morning.

TERESA MADE BRIAN breakfast, then took a quick shower, and got dressed before driving him across town.

"I'll be at Ms. Geddes's house working today." Teresa pulled up in front of the house.

"I thought you weren't going to work as much on Saturdays anymore."

Teresa cast a glance in his direction. "I'm helping her fix a barn door."

"Can't she do it herself?"

"Brian, not everyone is good at carpentry, and it takes the right tools."

"Oh."

"And remember..." She kissed the top of his head. "If you guys change your plans, call me and let me know."

The front door opened, and Steven stepped out onto the steps followed by his dad.

"I know," Brian said, with a touch of exasperation in his voice. "Bye, T." Eager to join his friend, he jumped out of the truck and shut the door. He ran a couple of steps then turned around and waved to Teresa.

After dropping Brian off, Teresa thought about picking up something to eat on the way to Maddy's house but decided it would make her late.

As it was, she arrived at Maddy's a few minutes after ten. She climbed out of her truck and opened the tailgate. Thankfully, to save time, she had loaded the tools she needed for the job the night before. The sun rising over the roof of the house bathed everything it touched in a golden brilliance.

Teresa turned when she heard the crunch of footsteps on the gravel driveway. The sunlight glinted over Maddy's figure as she walked out of the shade provided by the barn. There was a picture here, Teresa was sure.

"Good morning." Maddy greeted her with a cup of coffee. "I saw you pull into the driveway."

"Thanks." Teresa took the mug and inhaled the fresh aroma. "This smells wonderful."

Maddy laughed and inclined her head toward her apartment. "I have some muffins inside if you're interested. A little bird told me you don't always eat breakfast," she added quickly when Teresa raised an eyebrow.

"Oh, he did, did he? I don't always skip breakfast, but I won't turn down the offer of food, either."

Teresa followed Maddy up the stairs that led to the apartment over the barn. In the ample living room, a soft gold color adorned the walls. It reminded Teresa of the color maple leaves turned early in the fall. She admired the exposed rough-hewn beams that crossed the ceiling from one end to the other.

Filled with soft pillows, a couch separated the kitchen from the living area. When she walked past it, Teresa couldn't help but run her fingers over the soft chenille blanket with lush red, green, and blue colors that was draped invitingly over its back.

Two lamps with delicately carved wooden bases sat on mission style end tables at either side of the couch. Positioned across from the couch was a leather chair, with a stack of books and magazines piled beside it on the floor.

A wood-burning stove sat in a corner of the room on a base of tumbled stone and completed Maddy's well-used reading room.

Paintings of rugged landscapes and wildlife, some beautifully captured in oils and several others in watercolors, decorated the walls.

Teresa could smell a hint of roses in the air, and something that stirred memories from her childhood.

In the kitchen, Maddy opened the oven door and pulled a plate of muffins out with a gloved hand.

"I love what you've done in here."

"Thank you." A smile lit up Maddy's features. "I figured it was good practice for when the house is done. Come on in and sit."

Teresa complied and carefully set her coffee down on the table. She looked at the muffins Maddy offered to her. They were blueberry, her favorite.

"Thank you." She took one and bit into its warm softness. "I think this is the best muffin I've ever eaten."

"Or you're just very hungry." Maddy gave a soft laugh that made Teresa's insides quiver as if someone had just nibbled the nape of her neck.

She took a gulp of coffee in an attempt to hide her nervousness and then gathered her wits about her. "How's the school year starting out for you?"

"Good." Maddy pulled her muffin apart and popped a small piece into her mouth. "There're a couple of kids who are going to be tough nuts to crack, but I think they'll come around eventually."

"I don't know how you handle twenty six-year-olds in one room all day." Teresa took another bite of her muffin.

"Some days are more challenging than others. It's all about setting out what the expectation is for them. Once they know the rules, they generally want to follow them."

The sunlight streamed in the windows, and Teresa noticed little golden flecks in Maddy's deep indigo blue eyes. She studied them curiously until Maddy raised an eyebrow, and Teresa realized she was staring.

Maddy didn't seem embarrassed or uncomfortable by Teresa's scrutiny, instead she tilted her head and looked directly into Teresa's eyes with a bemused smile.

Teresa quickly stood up from the table. "So, are you ready to tackle that barn door?"

"The door?" Maddy laughed softly and then took another sip of her coffee. "Yes, I am."

THE MOST DIFFICULT part of the task was getting the door off its hinges. After finally freeing the last hinge pin, Teresa used one of the worktables and clamps that Rich left at the work site to secure the door, so she could go to work on it.

Maddy, Teresa discovered, was a fast learner and took over using the plane after Teresa used a marker to show her how much of the wood to shave off.

"So, what do you think of the construction so far?" Teresa scrubbed a wire brush diligently over one of the rust-covered hinges.

"I wish I could be here more during the day to see the process. Without the drywall up, it's hard to imagine what the rooms are going to look like."

"You've got a ways to go on the house yet. The electrical and plumbing rough-ins need to be completed and inspected. Then we can put insulation and drywall up. After that, we'll be able to make all the final connections and install all the surface plumbing and lighting fixtures."

"I suppose things will slow down at that point." Maddy stopped and inspected her work for a moment.

"They will, but the good thing is that all the major construction will be done, and we can bring in the painters and then have the flooring installed. The only thing after that will be to do some minor trim work."

Teresa set her wire brush down and took a moment to study Maddy's profile. Maddy intrigued Teresa. Here was a woman who was as comfortable wearing feminine sundresses and teaching children as she was working outside sanding a door in the hot sun, apparently unconcerned with how she looked or if she chipped a nail.

"How're you doing on the door?"

"I'm almost to the line you drew."

"Let me know when you're there, and then we'll reset the hinges." Teresa picked up another hinge and set to work cleaning it.

"So what do you do with your free time, Maddy?"

"It depends. Most nights I'm working on lesson plans, or reading, or if the mood strikes me, cooking." Maddy scraped the hand tool along the grain of the wood a few more times. She sat back with a sigh and wiped her arm across her forehead. "Angela doesn't live too far from here, so I visit her on the weekends."

"That must be nice having her nearby."

"It can be, but she tends to take after my mother. She's a worrier. Sometimes, she needs a reminder that I'm not a kid anymore. How about you, Teresa?"

Teresa wasn't used to having someone ask about her life, and she hesitated as she gathered her thoughts.

"During the week, when I get home early enough, Brian likes to help me make dinner. His mom was a great cook, and he was always in the kitchen asking questions. I want him to still have that." Teresa smiled sadly, and she hesitated a moment as her emotions got the better of her.

"David used to take him fishing, so we sometimes walk down to the pond in the evening, or in the morning, if I can roust him out of bed early enough, and just toss a couple of lines in. It's a riot to see how excited he gets when he actually catches a fish. Rich and Betty are like family, so we go over there a couple of times a month for dinner or to a cookout. Brian looks forward to spending time with them, so we make it a priority."

Teresa looked up to find Maddy watching her contemplatively.

"It sounds like you have a nice relationship with Brian."

"It's better now," Teresa said. "It wasn't in the beginning. Everything in Brian's life changed in one instant, and at the time, I was in shock and had no idea what to expect. We went through a lot together—some good, some trying, and some very difficult times. I think we've finally gotten to a place where we've settled into something that works for both of us."

Teresa paused, meeting Maddy's eyes. "Looks like you're finished shaving that down."

Maddy's voice faltered a bit. "I think we're ready to put those hinges back on."

It took about thirty minutes to reset the hinges and wrestle the door back into place. With Maddy's help, Teresa secured the door and then checked to make sure it was hanging level.

"That should do it." She stood back to inspect their work.

While Teresa packed her tools, Maddy tested the door.

"I could hardly open it before." She gently swung the door

back and forth a few times. "This is great, Teresa. Thank you."

"You're welcome." Teresa stood a few feet away from Maddy wishing there was a reason for her to stay longer.

Maddy looked over her shoulder as Teresa was watching her.

"I should go. I have to pick up Brian."

Maddy shut the barn door and walked over to where Teresa was standing. Maddy leaned in toward Teresa and then quickly stopped and stepped back. "I guess I'll see you Monday."

It took a moment for Teresa to recover from what she had hoped was about to happen between them and remember that she would be picking Brian up after Maddy tutored him. "Yes, yes, you will. I'll be there."

Teresa opened the door to her truck.

"Tell Brian I said 'hi.'"

"I will." Teresa climbed up into the front seat.

MADDY WATCHED HER drive down the gravel road. Teresa stuck an arm out the window and waved as she reached the bend in the road.

As she returned the gesture, Maddy decided that she genuinely liked Teresa. Teresa was a good-looking woman. Underneath the baggy work shorts, scuffed work boots, and rumpled T-shirt, if Maddy was any judge, was a strong, athletic body. Up close, she could see the sadness in those hazel eyes, definitely something soft and vulnerable beneath the guarded exterior Teresa allowed her to see. When she had stood near Teresa, her attention had shifted to Teresa's lips, and before she caught herself, Maddy almost acted on an impulse to kiss them.

Yet she had the feeling that on some level she made Teresa nervous. She stood in the yard watching the trail of dust settle until long after Teresa was gone, wondering what might have happened if she had kissed her.

Chapter
Seven

IT WAS MADDY'S free period on Tuesday afternoon, and she was relieved to have it since she spent her lunch helping one of the teachers with a new computer program. A knock on her door drew her attention from her work.

"Hi, Betty."

"Hi, yourself. I heard Mitch corralled you into helping him learn the new software program he got for his resource room.

Maddy set her pen down. "It wasn't that big of a deal."

"Just be warned, he has a habit of getting the new staff to help him out *a lot*. Don't let him take advantage of you. Here, we ordered pizza for lunch today. I saved you a couple of slices."

"Oh, that was thoughtful of you."

Betty pulled a chair over and sat across from Maddy. "How's everything going with your class so far?"

Maddy lifted the slice of pizza from the plate. "Good. I think the kids are starting to settle into a comfortable routine."

"That's nice to hear. How about you?"

Maddy bit into the pizza and then wiped the corners of her mouth with a napkin.

It had occurred to Betty that she knew very little about Maddy, and since the teacher was tutoring her favorite little boy, it was only right she wanted to know more about her. She had never heard Maddy mention children, a husband, or a boyfriend, and there were no pictures on her desk to offer any clues.

"This is good pizza."

"It's from Romanelli's."

"I'll have to remember that."

"So, how are you doing?" Betty asked. "I haven't had time to catch up with you since school started."

"Good. Busy. I haven't done much outside of teaching school and keeping up with the progress on the house."

"It's going well?"

"Everything's going according to schedule. Rich has warned

me that things will slow down once they start working on the inside."

"It's inevitable. Either there's a delivery that doesn't come in on time or an inspection that gets postponed, and an entire week goes by without any work getting done." Betty set her pizza aside. "Teresa Parker told me you're tutoring Brian."

"I started working with him last Monday." She wasn't sure, but for an instant, Maddy thought Betty's eyes misted with tears.

"How's he doing?"

"He's working hard. Brian is a good kid. It's hard to believe he lost both his parents two years ago."

"I'm glad he has you as a teacher." Betty opened a bottle of soda. "It was terrible, certainly something that no child should ever have to go through. Teresa lost her brother and became an instant parent in the span of one day. It's taken a long time, but Brian's finally starting to act like the little boy I knew before his parents died."

Maddy paused before taking another bite of her pizza. "What about Teresa?"

Betty sat back and deliberately met Maddy's gaze. "She's a wonderful person. Teresa's like a sister to me. She had a tough time of it after Brian came to live with her. When something of this magnitude happens, you find out pretty quickly who your friends are."

"It's difficult to lose friendships you thought would always be there."

"Yes, it is." Betty looked at her watch and stood up. "Listen, the reason I came by was to invite you over on Saturday. Rich and I are having a cookout. Brian and Teresa will be there. If you're free, why don't you come by the house? We'd love to have you."

"That sounds like fun. What time?"

"Anytime after noon."

"I'll be there. Thanks for the pizza, Betty."

"You're welcome." Betty winked at Maddy and walked out of the classroom.

MADDY FOUND HERSELF thinking about Teresa frequently throughout the week. She wasn't able to talk with her on Monday. Teresa had to straighten out a problem with a delivery, so Betty drove Brian home instead.

When she walked Brian out of school on Wednesday, she was disappointed again when Teresa's designated neighbor, Rose, was there to pick up Brian.

It wasn't until Friday afternoon when Maddy drove home and saw Teresa's red truck parked by a delivery of roof shingles that things changed.

Curious, Maddy ascended the steps into her new house. She let her eyes adjust to the natural light as she listened to the high-pitched whine of a saw cutting through wood followed a few seconds later by the tapping of a hammer.

"Teresa?" Maddy carefully climbed the staircase that led to the second floor. "Teresa?"

Off in one of the corners, Maddy saw Teresa hammering a nail into a piece of wood. When she was done, Teresa sat back on her haunches, the hammer in her right hand, resting on her thigh. She lifted a pair of safety goggles off her face.

"I thought I heard my name. I wasn't sure."

Maddy carefully stepped over a pile of two-by-fours and walked over to Teresa. "You're working late."

Teresa put her hand on the two-by-four she had just secured in place and pulled on it. "The plumber is supposed to start on Monday. I wanted to make sure the framing was done for the shower."

"I see the rest of the shingles got delivered."

"We'll finally be able to finish the garage roof next week."

"That's great. Where's Brian?"

"Oh, Rich and Betty are having him sleep over. We're having a cookout with them tomorrow, so they offered to take him tonight."

Maddy hesitated. An idea crept into her head, and she made a quick decision. "So, what do you do with a night off, besides work late?"

Teresa climbed to her feet. "Go home, take a shower, and catch up on some sleep."

Maddy clucked her tongue in disapproval. "I thought so."

"What's that?" Teresa slid her hammer into her tool belt.

"You left out dinner."

"I usually pick up something on the way home."

"Why don't you stay and have dinner with me? Nothing fancy. Just hamburgers and a salad."

"Okay."

"Good. I'll light the grill while you finish up in here. I'll leave the door unlocked, just come on up."

MADDY DISAPPEARED DOWN the stairs, and from the second floor window, Teresa watched her walk across the yard. Maddy stopped at the corner of the barn, pulled the gas grill out a few feet, and lit it.

Teresa shook her head, faintly amused and perplexed at her answer. The polite refusal had been on her lips, so she couldn't imagine why she heard herself accept the invitation. She wasn't even sure it was her voice for a moment. Then she thought about it. What could it hurt?

They were obviously both attracted to each other; at least she thought that was the case. They had been on the verge of a kiss last Saturday, but something had made Maddy back away and try to pretend that nothing had happened. In light of that, Teresa began to wonder if she had been wrong about Maddy's feelings for her. Teresa hoped that wasn't true because she genuinely liked Maddy.

She carried several things outside and locked them in the metal storage box in the back of her truck. She walked around to the passenger side and pulled out a pair of sneakers she kept handy. After changing into them, she tossed her boots onto the passenger side floor, brushed the sawdust from her clothes, and walked toward Maddy's apartment.

Teresa climbed up the flight of stairs and knocked lightly on the open door before she stepped through the threshold.

"Hi, come on in." Maddy walked across to the small pantry and pulled out a bottle of red wine.

"Can I use your bathroom to wash up?"

"Sure. It's up that one step, the first door on the left." She got down two glasses and set them on the counter.

MADDY POURED THE deep, red wine into one of the glasses while Teresa disappeared into the bathroom. She took a sip and then lifted the ground beef she had been defrosting out of the refrigerator. She hoped to satisfy some of the curiosity she had about Teresa Parker before the cookout tomorrow.

"Can I help with anything?" Teresa asked when she returned from the bathroom.

"You can be on salad duty." Maddy pulled lettuce and some other vegetables from the refrigerator and stacked them on the counter. "I poured some red wine. Would you like some?"

"Yes, thanks."

Maddy handed Teresa a knife and a cutting board. "You can start cutting up the tomatoes."

Maddy poured wine into a second glass and set it on the counter beside Teresa.

"How's Brian doing with the assignments I've given him?"

"Pretty good. He tries everything on his own. If he really gets stuck, I'll help him out." While Teresa cut up the tomatoes, Maddy began to wash the lettuce.

"Brian likes to learn," Maddy said, "and you're interested in what he does. That counts for a lot." She dried the lettuce in a spinner and drained the water off in the sink.

"I wish it could count for more."

"Don't be so hard on yourself. Brian's a strong boy, and he's got a good support system." Maddy opened the package of ground beef and formed two patties, which she set on a plate. She washed her hands and then retrieved a bag of hamburger buns from the refrigerator.

Teresa peeled an onion and cut thin slices onto the cutting board. "He's adjusting to life now, in his own way. I am, too, but it's different for me. I lost my brother. Brian lost the two most important people in his life."

"It doesn't seem natural," Maddy said. "I mean, when we're older, we've learned that death is part of the cycle of life. I guess the best we can do is make our peace with that knowledge and live our lives, because we know it will inevitably affect all of us."

"That doesn't mean you're ever prepared for it."

"No, it doesn't." Maddy picked up the plate. "I'm going to put the hamburgers on the grill. Why don't you come with me?"

Teresa set her knife down and rinsed her hands.

"I can't imagine what the past couple of years have been like for you."

"The first year was hell. Fran's parents filed a custody suit for Brian a week after the funeral. Thank God, David had spelled everything out in his will."

"That must have been awful to deal with."

"It was. The worst part was knowing that two people who hadn't been very involved in Brian's life to that point wanted to take him away from the only people he knew well."

"Did you ever want kids?"

Apparently caught off guard by the question, Teresa stared at Maddy.

"That was uncalled for, I'm sorry."

"It's all right. I've asked that question of myself many times." Teresa took a drink of the wine and followed Maddy down the stairs. "Where I was in my life, where I was going would never have led to having children. Now that I have Brian, I can't imagine not having him in my life."

"I doubt your brother would have made you Brian's guardian if he didn't see that maternal side of you while you were growing up." Maddy opened the grill and set the burgers on the hot grate.

Teresa blinked and managed a harsh laugh. "I think I need more wine for this conversation."

"I'm sorry. Am I asking too many questions?"

"What? No, just about things I haven't thought about in a long time."

"Go on." Maddy prompted her in a gentle voice after a minute of silence.

Teresa took another sip of wine. "My father walked out on my mother when I was ten. David was eight, and I can still see the look in his eyes when my mother sat us down and told us Dad wasn't coming home. Mom went to work full time, and David became my responsibility."

"You raised him."

"I guess you could call it that. We looked out for each other."

Maddy flipped the burgers. "Do you want your roll toasted?"

"Yeah, that sounds good."

"What happened with Brian's grandparents?"

"Rich and Betty found a lawyer for me, and we started the process so I could adopt him. His grandparents contested the will in court, but the judge thankfully upheld my brother and sister-in-law's wishes. The grandparents have visitation rights, but since they've moved to Arizona, they haven't come back to see him."

"I don't understand why they would go through all that and then not even bother to visit Brian."

"Fran was their only daughter. I think, in the end, it was just too painful a reminder of everything they lost."

"Families do some crazy things, don't they?"

"That's a kind way of putting it. They were out of their minds with grief. I guess at the time, that justified their idea of uprooting Brian from his environment and the only people he spent considerable time with outside of his mom and dad." Teresa looked at Maddy over the rim of her wineglass.

Maddy took the hamburgers and rolls off the grill and turned the burners off. "We're done out here. Why don't we go in and finish putting the salad together?"

OVER DINNER, THEIR conversation continued, and Maddy was getting a sense of Teresa. What she saw was someone with a clear perception of her responsibility to Brian, someone who had dealt with the shock, heartache, and anger that comes with an unexpected, tragic loss, and who, after everything, still provided a good home for Brian. It was obvious that he adored Teresa and was very comfortable with her. Together they were a family.

Maddy envied that. Christine had been her lover, but there was never a feeling of them being a family. Looking back, maybe that was what had been missing all along.

"Dinner was great, Maddy," Teresa said, as she leaned back in her chair.

"Thanks. It's so much more interesting to cook for more than just myself. I'm glad you enjoyed it." Maddy picked up her wineglass and swirled the red liquid around before finishing it. She liked the way Teresa carried her body with the grace of someone who was physically strong and yet still had the soft curves and sexy smile that were all so distinctly feminine. She couldn't help the growing attraction she felt.

"Let me help you get the dishes out of the way." Teresa stood and collected the plates from the table.

Maddy finally mustered the courage to pose the question she had been wondering how to ask for most of the evening. "What time are you going to Rich and Betty's tomorrow?"

"Probably around twelve." Teresa answered automatically, but then stopped on her way to the sink, and looked back at Maddy. "Wait. Are you going?"

Maddy broke into an embarrassed smile and carried two bowls past Teresa to the sink. "Betty asked me on Tuesday. I've been sitting here wondering if you would…if you would mind if I go."

Teresa set the plates down on the counter. "Why on earth would it be a problem?"

Maddy set her hands on the sink and blew out a sigh. "They're your friends, and I don't want to intrude on that."

"I don't consider it intruding. Betty invited you as her friend. You should be there, and besides, it would be nice to add to my small circle of friends."

Friends. The word stuck in Maddy's mind. *I wonder if we're even on the same page. Oh, Maddy, you might just be deluding yourself.* "I think that would be nice, too," Maddy said to cover the sudden pang of disappointment she felt.

Teresa helped her put the dishes in the dishwasher, even though Maddy insisted she could do it herself. Teresa checked her watch when they finished cleaning up the kitchen and putting the dishes away.

"I need to get going, Maddy. I promised Betty I would marinate some shrimp for tomorrow. Thanks again for dinner. It was great."

"Thanks for coming over." Frustrated with the direction of her thoughts, Maddy walked Teresa to the door. It made sense, though. Why would Teresa even contemplate a sexual encounter with someone who was her son's teacher?

"Good night, Teresa."

"I'll see you tomorrow."

When she closed the door, Maddy rested her head against the wood and rocked her head from side to side in utter frustration. *Oh, girl, you are in trouble here.*

Chapter
Eight

LATE SATURDAY MORNING, Teresa drove over to Rich and Betty's house on the other side of town. The lakefront property had been in Rich's family for generations. The freshwater lake, twenty-feet deep in spots, was stocked annually with trout.

Teresa always looked forward to the time she and Brian spent in the quiet community.

Brian loved to swim and would spend hours swinging from the rope Rich had secured to a large branch of a one-hundred-year-old oak tree that overhung the lake's edge.

Teresa parked behind Rich's truck and climbed out, shutting the door behind her. She lifted a cooler from the back of her vehicle and carried it up the front steps.

"Hello, anybody home?" she called through the screen door.

A moment later Betty walked to the door and opened it. "Come on in. Isn't it beautiful today?"

"You couldn't ask for nicer weather." Teresa stepped inside, set the cooler down, and gave Betty a hug. "There's shrimp and beer in the cooler."

"Perfect."

"Where are Rich and Brian?"

"They're out at the dock." Betty pointed toward the lake. "I told Rich he had to replace those rotten boards before our guests arrive today. He's been working on it all morning."

"I'll go see if I can give him a hand."

Betty rolled her eyes. "You're not working today. Sit and relax. I invited Madeline Geddes, too. Isn't she a wonderful teacher?"

Teresa couldn't help the smile that crossed her lips. "I know Brian likes her. Do you need any help in the kitchen?"

"No, Brian already offered to help me."

Teresa raised a curious eyebrow. "There must be some of your famous pies involved if he's hanging around the kitchen."

"Don't worry, Brian knows how to mind his manners. I'll take the shrimp off your hands. Are you okay carrying that cooler around back?"

"No problem." Teresa opened the cooler and handed Betty a gallon-sized plastic bag filled with marinated shrimp. "Here."

"Mmm, they look delicious. Now, what do I do, just put them on skewers?"

"Yeah."

"That's easy enough. Let me get the door for you."

Outside, Teresa walked to the edge of the lawn where the dock started and set the cooler down under a tree. "Do you need a hand, Rich?"

Rich's sun-tanned face appeared over the edge of the dock, and he flashed Teresa a grin. "Just a cold beer."

"I've got some here in the cooler." She jabbed her thumb over her shoulder. Teresa crouched at the edge of the dock and studied Rich's handiwork. "Nice job. It looks solid."

"It ought to be." He grunted as he lifted himself out of chest-deep water and climbed onto the dock. "I spent all morning replacing the wood."

Where's Brian?"

"He's out on the float. See him?"

Brian waved back at Teresa and then dove into the water. He surfaced a second later and started to swim toward the dock.

Rich and Teresa both looked toward the driveway when they heard the spit of gravel.

"I should get the grill started, or we'll be eating late." Rich reached for a towel draped over a lounge chair.

"Here, I'll get this stuff back to the shed, so it's out of the way."

It took only a few minutes to load the broken pieces of the rotten two-by-fours into a wheelbarrow and to gather the tools.

Teresa was closing the shed door when Brian climbed up the ladder. He wrapped her in a wet hug just as she turned around.

"Ugh. Thanks Brian. I guess you're having a good time." She ruffled his hair.

"Awesome. Hey, look who's here." He pointed past Teresa's shoulder. "Hi, Ms. Geddes."

Teresa watched as Betty and Maddy walked over to Rich.

"Hi, Brian. You look like you're having fun," Maddy said.

He nodded enthusiastically before he grabbed a towel from one of the chairs and wrapped it around himself. His teeth chattered, and he leaned against Teresa for a minute while she rubbed his back.

"Nice to see you again, Madeline." Rich shook her hand.

"Likewise. Please call me Maddy. And thanks for inviting me."

"Our pleasure, Maddy. Well, I'm going to get washed up."

Rich trotted off toward the house, leaving the three women standing together.

"Hello again," Teresa said, as she looked at Maddy.

Maddy returned Teresa's gaze, her blue eyes smiling with apparent affection at her. "Hi, Teresa." She turned her attention to Brian. "You're shivering."

"No, I'm getting warm," he said as he fought off a shiver and a bout of chattering teeth.

"It'll be a little while before we're ready to eat," Betty said. "I'm going to get a couple of things done in the kitchen, so you two just enjoy yourselves." Brian threw off his towel and trotted after Betty.

Teresa caught a glimpse of Maddy's profile. A headband pulled her hair back from her face, and she wore a casual outfit of neatly pressed jeans and a lime green T-shirt. She let her gaze drift to Maddy's inviting full lips, her breasts, and then quickly tracked back up to her face just as Maddy turned and seemed to study Teresa's expression.

The warm, intimate gaze sent a sensual jolt directly down to her groin. For a moment, neither one said anything. After a moment, Maddy spoke. "I would love to know what on earth you were thinking just then."

Teresa straightened and tucked her hands into her pockets as she tried to find a way out of the perilous position she had created for herself.

"Daydreaming, I suppose."

"Hey, Teresa, watch me!"

She turned, pitifully grateful for the distraction, and watched Brian race past them. He bounded off the dock, grabbed the rope in midair, and swung out over the water. As he reached the peak of his arc, he released the rope, somersaulted into the lake, and sent up a plume of water.

"Wow, he's quite the acrobat," Maddy said. Brian's head popped up from beneath the water, and he climbed up the ladder and shook himself like a dog.

"Do you swim?" Teresa asked. The heat of the moment had passed, but Teresa couldn't stop thinking about what it might be like to kiss Maddy Geddes.

"I used to, but I hardly get the chance anymore."

"Sounds like you miss it."

"I do. Standing here brings back some childhood memories," Maddy said, with a hint of longing in her voice.

"And simpler times, I imagine," Teresa added softly with a wistful smile.

Maddy returned the smile, and Teresa felt a strange fluttering inside her chest. She suddenly found it difficult to focus on anything apart from the curve of Maddy's mouth, her full lips, and the dimples that formed her bright smile.

From across the yard, Rich opened the door and stepped out of the house with a tray full of skewered shrimp. "Now, how about that beer?"

"Here." Teresa dug a cold beer out of the ice and handed it to him. "Maddy, there's wine and soda in there, too, if you're interested," Teresa said, suddenly grateful for Rich's presence.

"Thanks, I brought some red wine along for Betty to try."

Betty soon appeared, carrying a tray of glasses and a pitcher of freshly brewed iced tea that she set on the picnic table.

"Rich, can you get the corn? It's on the kitchen table. Where's Brian?" Betty turned around looking for him.

"Over here," Brian called as he climbed up the ladder and grabbed a dry towel.

"You can go with Uncle Rich and bring the plates out."

"On my way." Rich tipped his beer in salute, set it on the picnic table, and walked away from the group.

"How's the house coming along, Maddy?" Betty asked.

"Great. I know I'm ahead of myself, but I can't wait to see it finished."

"The outside always goes quickly. You've got to figure about three to four months before everything's done," Teresa said.

"Just keep reminding me of that perspective when I get impatient."

"Not that I'm biased or anything, but you have two of the best people building it for you," Betty said.

Rich returned, carrying a brown bag filled with corn. Tagging along behind him, Brian balanced a tray of plates in his hands. "Ooh, did I hear a compliment being tossed our way by my wife, T?"

"I believe so, Rich." Teresa relieved Brian of the plates and set them on the table. "Thanks, kiddo."

"Mind yourself, Rich. You still have to fit through that door at the end of the day," Betty said, teasing.

Teresa snickered as she laid the skewered shrimp out on the grill.

Maddy stood on the other side of the grill and sipped her glass of red wine. "Mmm, those shrimp smell delicious."

"Teresa won't admit it, but she's actually quite a good cook." Betty wrapped an arm around Brian conspiratorially and led him off toward the dock.

"A woman of varied talents," Maddy mused as she raised her glass to her lips again.

"I suppose you could say that." Teresa felt a flush rising on her cheeks. She quickly turned over the skewers and took a swig of beer. "Hey, you guys, don't disappear. The shrimp will be done in a couple of minutes."

Betty and Brian sauntered back to the table with self-satisfied grins plastered on their faces.

"Everyone sit and start with the shrimp," Betty said. "We've got steak and chicken for later." She wrapped the towel tightly around Brian's shoulder and guided him to one side of the table, leaving Teresa to sit next to Maddy.

"What were you two up to over there?" Teresa raised a suspicious eyebrow as she removed the shrimp from the grill.

"That's for us to know and for you to find out." Betty took the plate from Teresa and set it in the middle of the table.

"Lord, I don't like the sound of that." Teresa paused, then sat down on the picnic bench and accepted the plate of shrimp that Maddy handed to her. "Thanks."

Betty poured the iced tea into the glasses and passed them around the table. When she stepped behind Rich and handed him his glass, he captured her hand and kissed her palm lightly.

"Thanks, Betty."

A blush crept up Betty's face as she sat down next to him.

Teresa stole a glance at Maddy and caught her looking at Betty and Rich with a wistful smile playing around the corners of her mouth. Teresa saw the affection that Rich and Betty felt for each other reflected in their eyes. Something about that must have struck a chord with Maddy.

Teresa couldn't remember the last time someone had looked at her like that. Even Erin had never looked at her with that open and unguarded expression.

"Hey, Uncle Rich, do you have fireworks we can set off later?"

"Brian, it's not polite to ask," Teresa chided him in a low voice.

"It's okay, T. I made sure to stock up just for the occasion." Rich winked at Brian from across the table.

"And here I thought I only had one boy sitting at the table tonight." Betty said.

"The last time we shot off fireworks was over a year ago—" Rich grunted as Betty unceremoniously elbowed him in the ribs. "Sorry, Teresa."

"Don't worry about it. It's water under the bridge."

"Time for me to get the meat on the grill." Rich stood up from the table.

"I'll help." Brian jumped up from the table and ran after him.

"Men, they have no tact sometimes," Betty said.

"Rich certainly didn't mean anything by it. Besides, it's Erin's loss at this point, not ours."

"Good girl." Betty raised her glass of iced tea and clinked it against Teresa's beer bottle. "Maddy, will you stay for the fireworks? Rich shoots them off over the lake, so it really is quite safe."

"I'd love to."

Teresa was quiet as she took a bite of shrimp and chewed it.

LATER, AFTER EVERYONE had eaten their fill of barbecued chicken and steak, Teresa cleared the paper plates from the picnic table and dumped them into a garbage can. She shooed Betty away from the kitchen.

"You cooked. I can do the clean up."

"I'll help, too." Maddy collected the plate of leftover chicken from the table. "It'll go faster that way."

Teresa held the door for Maddy and followed her into the kitchen.

Maddy set the plate down on the counter and turned to Teresa. "Dinner was fantastic."

"Yes, it was," Teresa said. *I think the company had a lot to do with that.*

Teresa silently chastised herself. This was Brian's teacher, and any thoughts of anything else were completely inappropriate.

This thing she was feeling was a ridiculous crush, and she needed to put a stop to it right now. But it was no use. All her mind would focus on throughout dinner was the nearness of Maddy's body, and the beautiful hands with short, well-manicured nails that had fleetingly touched her arm during the casual conversation over their meal.

"Betty and Rich seem as though they're very happy together," Maddy said. She found a Tupperware container in one of the cabinets.

Teresa pulled her thoughts together as she turned on the faucet at the sink. "They're a great couple and good friends." She set to work washing the bowls and utensils.

"Who was Erin?" Maddy asked in a casual tone.

Teresa cocked her head and stared down at the running water. "She was the woman I lived with for five years. After six months of Brian being with us, Erin decided that being a parent wasn't what she had in mind for herself, so she left."

"I'm so sorry, Teresa." Maddy stepped between Teresa and the kitchen table, lightly touching Teresa on the small of her back with her free hand as she squeezed past her.

Teresa's breath caught somewhere in her throat, and she felt a quiver of excitement in the pit of her belly all out of proportion from the innocent touch.

"Teresa?" Maddy was looking at her as she shut the refrigerator door. "Are you okay? I'm sorry. I didn't mean to dredge up bad memories for you."

"You didn't." Teresa pulled herself together. "Don't get me wrong. Erin was a good person. What happened to Brian changed our lives, but I know I'm lucky to have Brian in my life."

"I think he's lucky to have you."

Teresa smiled. "That means a lot to me."

"I mean it. I can't imagine raising a child by myself, let alone under the circumstances you've had to deal with."

"I just want Brian to have some stability in his life. He's experienced so much loss at such a young age. I worry about him."

For a moment, neither of them said anything.

"Maddy, I—" Teresa looked at the floor and then back at Maddy. "I just wanted to say thank you."

"What for?" Maddy's voice sounded tight and strained.

"For helping Brian."

The door to the kitchen opened, and Brian stuck his head inside. "Uncle Rich is taking the boat out to the float to shoot off the fireworks. Can I go with him, Aunt T?"

"What's Betty doing?"

"She's staying on the dock."

"Stay with Aunt Betty. I don't want you that close to where the fireworks are being shot off."

"Please, Teresa. I promise I won't get close to them."

"Brian, I said no."

With an exasperated sigh, he hung his head and then ducked back outside. Teresa looked over at Maddy and shrugged. "He'll get over it."

"Oh, I know." Maddy walked to the back door. "Why don't we find a spot to watch the fireworks from?"

"Sounds good to me." Teresa dried her hands on a towel and laid it on the counter.

Outside, Betty met Teresa halfway across the yard. "I'll make you a compromise. I'll take Brian out on the boat, and I promise we'll stay away from where Rich is shooting off the fireworks."

Teresa chuckled. "Did he ask you, or did the two of you come up with this together earlier?"

"Shush, now." Betty swatted Teresa's arm.

Teresa held her hands out in surrender. "All right. He can go, but nowhere near the fireworks."

Betty turned around and gave Brian the thumbs up sign. He cheered and called out. "Come on, Aunt Betty!"

"I come bearing gifts," Maddy joked, as she lifted a bottle of wine and held two glasses in her other hand. "Can I interest you in a glass?"

"Absolutely. Come sit over here."

It was dark except for a few torches Rich had lit along the edge of the dock. Teresa sat on a wooden swing that faced out over the lake.

"It's beautiful out here," Maddy said quietly, as she joined her. "So, whose idea was it to go out on the boat?"

"Probably both of them."

"It's been years since I've seen fireworks." Maddy handed Teresa a glass.

"You're in for a treat then."

Teresa watched as Brian climbed into the boat. Betty waited until Brian sat down and then pushed the boat away from the dock with an oar. She easily maneuvered the boat past where Teresa and Maddy were sitting.

There was a high-pitched whine as Rich set off the first fireworks. They arched up over the lake and lit up the sky with bursts of green and blue lights intermingled with hints of red. For a moment, they seemed to pulse with life in the night sky before fading into the dark.

"Where does he get them?"

"He has connections, but don't ask him to tell you who they are."

"I guess that's privileged information."

Teresa took a sip of wine and set her glass down. "Look at the reflection off the lake."

The fireworks exploded into shimmering green that shifted and expanded into gold and blues. They sat on the swing and watched the show as it continued in the sky.

"When I was a kid," Maddy said, "my sister and I would find a spot as close to the Fourth of July fireworks as we could and lie on our backs to watch them."

"Sounds like fun." Teresa could barely see the boat, and she leaned against the back of the swing.

Maddy could feel the warmth of Teresa's body, and it stoked something inside her. She glanced out toward the float and saw the silhouette of the boat lit up under the lights from the other houses around the lake.

In the distance, she could hear Brian shouting in excitement as Rich sent off more fireworks.

"Teresa?"

"Mmm." Teresa pulled herself back from staring out at the reflection of the fireworks on the water. A playful smile crossed her lips as she gazed into Maddy's eyes.

Maddy swallowed and wondered if Teresa could hear her heart hammering loudly in her chest. She looked at Teresa and saw moonlight and desire reflecting in her eyes.

Teresa felt the distance between them melting away. She leaned in closer and brushed her warm lips against Maddy's, lingering a moment and then pulling away with a smile. "I've wanted to kiss you all day."

Maddy stroked the backs of her fingers against Teresa's cheek. Then she reached up, slid a hand into Teresa's hair, and pulled her closer. Her mouth touched Teresa's and glided in a long, slow exploration over her lips. Teresa's lips were soft, and there was a powerful rush of emotion in feeling them press against hers.

Maddy deepened the kiss, her mouth stroking and her tongue teasing Teresa's lips open. She explored tentatively with her tongue, and Teresa responded to the intimate kiss by wrapping her arms fiercely around Maddy and pulling her against her body.

The intensity of the kiss ignited a fire in Teresa's belly. She wanted to feel Maddy's strong body with its enticing curves, taste her lips, and inhale the heady scent of her perfume.

Maddy clasped Teresa to her, while Teresa's hands caressed the sides of her breasts and then slid down to cup her hips.

The boom of fireworks and the nearness of excited voices jerked Teresa back, and to Maddy's immediate disappointment, the kiss abruptly ended.

"They're not here yet." Maddy drew Teresa back while trying to recover her equilibrium. She didn't want to let go of the electrifying feeling that stirred deep inside her.

"I know," Teresa said. She rested her forehead against Maddy's. "Wow. I wasn't expecting that to happen."

Maddy cupped Teresa's cheek and slowly rubbed a thumb over her soft bottom lip. "I'm glad it did." Maddy slid her mouth across Teresa's cheekbone to her ear where she whispered, "I'm not used to this. It's been awhile since I've felt this way about someone." Her warm breath made Teresa shiver.

They pulled away and looked at each other for a moment. "Are you okay?" Maddy said.

"Yes," Teresa whispered. "I wanted to kiss you last night, but I thought it was too soon."

Maddy was intoxicated by Teresa's response, and she wanted to make her tremble again, only the next time to a long, slow orgasm. She knew she shouldn't rush things. They had barely known each other for a month.

The sounds of laughter and splashing water caught their attention. The rowboat glided closer to the dock.

"Brian...I have to take him home. It's his bedtime."

"I'm sure he's probably tired." Maddy forced her thoughts away from her carnal desires and onto Brian. She captured Teresa's hand and felt fingers curl around hers. She wanted to say, "Stay with me tonight," but knew it was selfish and wouldn't be fair to ask something that she knew Teresa wasn't prepared or able to give her yet.

Teresa squeezed Maddy's hand. "I don't know how or when I'll see you again. I have to think of Brian."

"I know you do. I'll see you Monday after school."

"Monday? Oh, geez. Yes, you're tutoring him. I think my brain just shut off."

Maddy suspected Teresa was in the same emotional and physical condition she was in, and she liked that. "Come on, I'll help you get your things together."

"Aunt T, Ms. Geddes! Weren't the fireworks cool?" Brian was breathless as he climbed out of the boat and ran across the dock.

"Yes, they were, Brian." He climbed up onto the swing and sat next to her. "Did you thank Uncle Rich and Aunt Betty for having you over?"

"Um..."

"Well, go say thank you. We need to get going in a few minutes."

"Can't we stay for a little while?"

"Brian, you've been here since yesterday. It's time to go home."

"Okay." He slid off the swing and trudged across the yard.

Some twenty minutes later, after collecting Brian's duffel bag and saying their goodbyes to Rich and Betty, Teresa and Maddy walked over to Teresa's truck.

"Goodnight, Ms. Geddes," Brian said, as he opened the passenger side door and climbed up into the seat.

"Goodnight, Brian." Maddy waved and then turned to Teresa.

"Until Monday," Teresa said, with a smile as they walked to the back of her truck.

"I'm not going to be able to think of anything else but you." Maddy was about to reach up and kiss Teresa, but she could see Brian watching them curiously through the rear window.

"Neither will I." Teresa dropped the duffel bag into the truck bed. She walked Maddy to her car and held the door open for her until she settled into the driver's seat.

Maddy started the engine of her Volkswagen Beetle, and waved to Teresa as she backed out of the driveway. She spent the drive home thinking about the fireworks over the lake and everything they had shared earlier that night.

Chapter
Nine

MONDAY MORNING ARRIVED with a clear autumn sky and cool breeze that rustled through the branches of the trees overhead. The first yellow and red hues were visible in the leaves of the sugar maples and red oaks that dotted the landscape.

Maybe the colors were more vivid this year. Teresa wasn't sure and couldn't recall last fall's foliage display to even consider that possibility. The more likely reason was she had hardly paid attention to the changing seasons after David and Fran died.

She clung to the routine she and Brian had adopted, and today, like any other, she was on the work site at ten to eight with steaming cups of coffee for her and Rich.

The losses in her life had sucked her dry for two years, left her feeling empty and hulled out. The past month, though, something was different. The grief was still there, but somehow not as razor-edge sharp in her chest.

She walked with her coffee in hand past the barn door that Maddy and she had spent part of a morning fixing. She came across a small vegetable garden on the other side of the barn where the morning sun lit up the yard.

She sipped her coffee while she looked with interest at the assortment of tomatoes, peppers, and herbs that were carefully fenced in to keep out the small animals. Something about seeing the garden and knowing that Maddy had planted and tended it made Teresa smile.

Behind her, she heard the rumble of Rich's diesel engine and wandered back around front.

"Boy, do I need that coffee today," Rich said as he climbed out of his truck.

"Late night?"

"Nah, I must be getting a lousy cold." He tugged the cup from its Styrofoam holder and surveyed the tarp they had secured over the garage the week before.

"I still can't believe they didn't deliver all the damn shingles the first time."

"Good thing we had enough to do the main roof." Teresa set up the fifteen-foot ladder against the garage. She cinched her tool belt around her waist, climbed up, and started to pull back the tarp. She stepped carefully around the roofing material that had been hoisted onto the garage roof in several strategic positions the day before. "Hey, are you going to help, or are you just sightseeing?"

"Nah, I'm coming."

"You could always call Nate and have him work here today."

"No, he's got a couple of subs working for him at the framing job."

"Let's get to it then. The sooner we get started the earlier you get out of here today," Teresa said.

"Yeah, there's no sense bitching about it."

Teresa finished removing the tarp and settled into the task of laying down and securing the drip edge, the underlayer of tarpaper, and the ice and water shield. She'd just finished stapling the first set in when Rich joined her on the roof.

They worked together securing the tarpaper to the plywood, and then started on the shingles. All morning long, the pounding of the pneumatic hammers echoed in the air in a rhythmic rat-a-tat-tat.

Teresa sat down on the roof to rest for a moment. She cast a curious glance over at her unusually quiet partner.

"You doing okay over there, Rich?"

Rich, kneeling with the hammer in his right hand resting on his thigh, shook his head.

"What's wrong?"

"I need to get down."

Teresa watched in dismay as the hammer slid from Rich's hand, and he crawled clumsily to the ladder.

"Rich!" Throwing caution to the wind, Teresa scrambled across the roof and grabbed his tool belt to steady him as he teetered precariously at the top of the ladder.

"I can't...catch...my breath."

"For God's sakes, don't climb down."

He brushed her hand away and slowly worked his body onto the ladder. "No."

Teresa could only hold the ladder as Rich awkwardly maneuvered his way down to the ground. When he was at the bottom, she fumbled with nervous fingers to unclip her cell phone from her belt. She flipped it open and dialed 911.

"What's your emergency?" the dispatcher asked.

"I need an ambulance. My partner's having a heart attack."

"Ma'am, what's you're address?"

"Twelve Spring Vale Road, Morristown."

"I'm sending help right away."

Teresa scrambled down the ladder and missed the bottom rung. She landed off balance and winced as her right ankle rolled in.

She limped over to where Rich was lying on the ground a few feet away. "Rich?"

He opened his eyes and looked at Teresa. "Nice landing."

She knelt down beside him and cradled his head in her lap. "Shut up and keep breathing."

From the time Teresa called the emergency operator to the moment she heard the wail of sirens in the distance and growing louder were the longest five minutes of her life. Barely aware of the ache in her ankle, she was terrified that Rich would fall unconscious or die before help arrived.

"They brought out the cavalry for you, Rich," Teresa said, as a police car followed by an ambulance pulled into the yard.

One of the paramedics grabbed a bag out of the ambulance and ran over to where Rich was lying.

"What happened?" he asked, as he crouched next to Teresa and set the bag down beside him.

"We were up on the roof working, and he said he couldn't catch his breath." Teresa watched him quickly assess Rich.

"You with me, buddy?" the paramedic asked, as he checked Rich's pulse.

"Feels like...a vice grip around...my chest."

"Hang in there. We're going to get you to the hospital." He motioned to his partners who quickly pulled the stretcher out of the back of the rig. "Danny, let's get a full set of vitals on him, so we can call them into the ER."

When the paramedic tore open a package containing an intravenous needle, Teresa stood up and hobbled a couple of steps away to give them room.

"What did you do to yourself?" the police officer asked.

"I twisted my ankle. It's nothing. I've done it before."

"Ma'am, it wouldn't hurt to get it checked out. Make sure nothing's broken."

"Sam, do you have enough room in there to take the lady, too?" he asked.

The first paramedic looked up at Teresa. "Yeah, we've got a seat for you in the back."

It was several minutes before they had Rich strapped onto the stretcher and lifted into the back of the ambulance.

When they finished securing him, the paramedics helped Teresa in and strapped her into the seat.

The police officer poked his head in the back. "Sam, the mobile intensive care unit will meet up with you on South Street."

"Thanks," he replied. The officer shut the door and the paramedic called to the driver. "Let's go."

As the sirens started, Teresa reached across and squeezed Rich on the shoulder. She lowered her head to hide the tears welling up in her eyes.

TERESA DETESTED HOSPITALS. Without warning, it brought her back to that awful day. She had been the one to identify her brother's body, and the memory still left her breathless just as the initial shock of seeing him had done to her almost three years ago. In the days and months that followed, the numbness began to wear off, and the grief, and anger coalesced into a dark depression.

She hadn't been able to break out of its icy grip. Sleep was an escape but it brought nightmares, and they were sometimes worse than being awake and looking into Brian's mournful eyes everyday.

She went to therapy and took the antidepressants and the sleeping pills for months. The pills wrapped her in a gauzy veil of numbness but did not change the awful reality of her life.

Now she sat in the hallway triage area unaware of the usual hospital noises: the squeak of rubber-soled shoes against the polished floors, the announcements and pages, the motorized noise of the double doors opening and closing as staff came and went from the emergency department. She tried her best to ignore the panicky feeling that threatened to overtake her. Her best friend had suffered a heart attack, and she had no idea what the future held for him.

She sat with her elbows on her knees, head in hands, staring down at her work boots in the terrible silence that occurs when a life hangs in the balance and one is helpless to do anything about it.

"Ms. Parker?"

Teresa became aware of tightness from the swelling around her right ankle inside her boot. She couldn't quite remember what she had done to it.

"Ms. Parker?"

She looked up and focused on the woman standing in front of her. She was wearing blue scrubs and bright pink clogs.

"Sorry, what?"

"Your friend would like to see you. He's awake and asking for you."

It all came roaring back: the roof, Rich collapsing, and Teresa holding onto him for dear life. "How is he?"

"He's stable now. His wife's with him. I can give you a couple minutes before they take him up to the cardiac care unit."

"Thanks." Teresa followed the nurse into the emergency department. The noise of monitors beeping, the sound of a baby crying, and the smell of antiseptic assaulted her senses.

She opened the curtain and stepped inside the booth. Rich lay on the bed hooked up to an oxygen mask and two intravenous lines. He looked small and vulnerable lying underneath the sheets. Betty looked up from where she was resting her head on the pillow next to Rich and held a hand out to Teresa.

"Thank God for you, Teresa." Betty stood up and wrapped her arms around her in a fierce hug.

"How is he?" Teresa stepped back from the hug and looked down at Rich.

"They're going to run some more tests, but they think he's going to be all right. Rich told me what you did."

"He would have done the same for me."

Rich opened his eyes and waved Teresa over with a shaky hand.

"Thanks. The doc said you saved my life, calling when you did."

Teresa squeezed his hand.

"Now it's your turn to take better care of it," Betty said to him. "Teresa, why are you limping? Did anyone look at your leg?"

"No, not yet. I—what time is it?"

"One-thirty," Betty replied.

"I came down the ladder too fast and twisted my ankle. I can take care of it at home."

"Don't you remember, you rode in the ambulance with Rich?"

"My truck. I guess I didn't plan that out too well."

"Nonsense." Betty opened the curtain and found Rich's nurse standing a few feet away. "Stacy, can you look at my friend's ankle?"

"Sure." She walked over and watched as Teresa took a limping step. "Let me get the doctor, so he can decide if he wants to have an X-ray taken."

"But what about Brian?" Teresa asked Betty.

"Don't worry." Betty turned her towards Stacy. "I'll make sure he's taken care of. Go get your ankle checked out."

TERESA SAT ON the exam table and checked her watch for what seemed like the hundredth time. She shivered as an air-conditioned breeze blew out of a ceiling vent.

Outside the door, she heard a male voice and watched as the handle on the door turned. A tall, thin man with blond hair walked in and cast a cursory glance at Teresa's face before focusing on her ankle.

"I'm Doctor Forman. You're very lucky, Ms. Parker." He slid the X-ray films into a box on the wall and then flipped a switch. The ghostly image of Teresa's right ankle and foot appeared when the light flickered on. "Just by looking at your ankle with the amount of bruising and swelling that you have, I would have bet that you had a fracture. But you don't. You have a sprain and a bone bruise."

"What do I do for that?" Teresa gingerly rubbed her discolored and swollen ankle.

"Unfortunately, nothing. Only rest and time will heal it." He removed a package from a cabinet behind him. "You need to wear this ace wrap until the swelling goes down."

A dismayed feeling rose in her as she watched the doctor quickly wrap her foot with the bandage. "Great. Well, at least it's not my right hand."

"You should follow up with an orthopedist in a week." He pulled out a small prescription pad and wrote quickly.

"What's an orthopedist going to do?"

"Make sure your ankle is healing properly, and there are no complications." He handed her the piece of paper. "That's an order for eight hundred milligrams of Motrin."

Teresa eyed him dubiously. "Thanks."

"Here are some crutches. Do you know how to use them?"

"Yeah, I've used them before."

"You should stay off that ankle for a few days. By the way, there's a young man here to see you. I wrote your discharge orders, so you're free to go."

"Thanks."

The door swung open and Brian charged into the room, followed by Maddy. "Aunt T, are you okay?"

"I'm fine," she assured him as he hugged her tightly. Teresa met Maddy's worried gaze over Brian's shoulder and grinned affectionately at her. "Thanks for bringing him here."

"Betty called the school and told me what happened. She said it would be okay with you if I brought Brian over."

"It's more than okay. It's good to see you both. Did you get to see Rich?"

"Only for a couple of minutes. They were taking him upstairs to a room on the cardiac floor."

"Is Uncle Rich going to be okay?"

Teresa hesitated. She knew better than to try to gloss over the seriousness of the situation with Brian.

"The doctors are going to run some tests to find out what's

wrong. He's in the best place he can be right now."

Brian regarded her quietly before he answered. "Can we come see him tomorrow?"

"We'll see how Uncle Rich is feeling. If he's up to it, I'm sure he'd love to see you." Teresa wrapped her arm around Brian's shoulders and kissed the top of his head.

"Okay," he said, seemingly satisfied. "Can we get something to eat? I'm starving."

Teresa sighed. "We will. Maddy, I'm afraid the work site is a mess. Both our trucks are there, and all the equipment is lying around on the ground. I'll call a couple of the guys we work with and get it cleaned up for you."

"I appreciate that, Teresa, but right now..." She handed Teresa the crutches and helped her stand up. "I'd really like to get you and Brian something to eat." Maddy reached out, picked up Teresa's boot, and handed it to Brian.

"Maddy you don't have to do that."

"I know, but I want to." She glanced back at Brian who was tagging along a couple of steps behind them. "Any requests, Brian?"

"Pizza!" He slung the boot over his shoulder and skipped a couple of steps.

"Then, pizza it is. What kind do you want?"

"Pepperoni and cheese."

"Teresa?"

"That's my favorite, too."

"That makes it easy." She flipped open her cell phone and called in their order as they walked out of the hospital.

"You have Romanelli's on speed dial?" Teresa asked when Maddy finished the call.

"Oh, yes. When I don't feel like cooking, it's the place I order from the most."

ON THE TEN-minute drive to Romanelli's, Brian peppered Teresa with questions about what had happened to Rich. He was fascinated that she got to ride in the ambulance with him. Maddy glanced over at Teresa in amusement as she answered each question.

When they arrived, Maddy held the door as Teresa maneuvered past her on her crutches and Brian followed. Inside, old-style world maps, some depicting the routes of Marco Polo and Columbus, decorated the walls.

Teresa leaned closer to Maddy. "We'll meet you at the table. I'm going to take Brian to the restroom."

"Are you sure? I can go with him if you like."

"It's okay. I want to wash up a bit before I eat. Something about hospitals and all those sick people."

"I'll get us a booth."

"Great."

Ten minutes later, Brian led the way as Teresa returned to the dining room on her crutches. The room was set for dinner, and there were plenty of patrons. Teresa recognized some familiar faces as she looked around for Maddy.

She was grateful to Maddy for the companionship and support she offered. Maddy let her deal on her own terms with the feelings that were stirred by the kiss they shared on Saturday, with no overtures of pressuring her.

She located Maddy sitting in a corner booth. It was a popular spot, and Teresa assumed that Maddy must have asked for it when she called in their order.

Maddy looked lost in her own thoughts. Her sorrowful expression caught Teresa by surprise. As she crossed the room, Teresa realized she'd never seen that side of Maddy before, and she wondered what caused it.

"Ms. Geddes," Brian called as he neared the booth.

Maddy drew herself back and smiled at both of them, erasing the sorrow from her expression

"You must have an 'in' here. You've got the best seat in the house."

Maddy sat back and folded her arms. "I have my connections."

Teresa motioned Brian into the booth. She leaned the crutches against the booth enclosure and slipped in beside him.

"Thanks for getting us dinner."

"You're welcome." Maddy looked up as a waitress arrived. "Hey, Abby."

"Hi, Maddy." The waitress, who looked to be barely out of high school, set down a glass of iced tea in front of her and pulled out her pad. "What can I get you two to drink?"

"Milk, please, for both of us," Teresa answered.

"Great. How's the house coming, Maddy?" Abby asked, as she collected the menus from the table.

"Good. You'll have to come over and see it when it's done."

"Love to. Your pizza will be out in a few minutes."

Maddy looked back at Teresa and Brian when Abby walked away. "Abby's student teaching at our school. She graduates in December."

"Teresa, can I go play a video game, please?"

She glanced over at the arcade games a few feet away. "Do you have quarters?"

"Yeah, I do."

Teresa stepped awkwardly out of the booth and let Brian get past. "I'll call you when the pizza comes."

Teresa sat down and looked across the table at Maddy. "What were you thinking about before I came over?"

An odd expression crossed Maddy's features. "Nothing, just spacing out."

"Looked more like brooding to me."

Maddy picked up her tea and cast her eyes down. Teresa knew that something had been bothering her, but she dropped the subject.

"So, do you make it a habit of taking care of people?"

Maddy set her glass down, gazed into the distance, and then looked back at Teresa. "No, just the ones I care about." She glanced up as Abby arrived with the pizza pan and set it down on the table.

"It's piping hot out of the oven." Abby pulled some extra napkins out of her apron and set them down on the table. She accepted two large glasses of milk from one of the waiters and placed them in front of Teresa.

"Thanks, Abby."

"You're welcome." She smiled at them and walked away.

Brian returned from his game-playing and scooted into the booth next to Teresa.

"Did you win?" she asked.

"I got the second highest score."

"Here." Teresa lifted up a slice of pizza that trailed a long stretched-out string of cheese behind it as she set it down on his plate.

He picked off a piece of pepperoni, blew on it, and popped it into his mouth. "Is Aunt Betty going to be at school tomorrow?"

Teresa pulled the cheese apart and ate it as she considered Brian's question. "Probably not. She'll stay at the hospital with Uncle Rich."

"I want to stay with her tomorrow."

"You have school, and the hospital is no place for you to be hanging out all day."

Brian fell silent as he ate.

Teresa had an idea about what was bothering Brian, but she kept it to herself. For months after his father and mother died, he would wake up at night crying hysterically. When she could get him to calm down and talk to her, she finally realized that he thought if he had been there when his mom and dad were hurt, they wouldn't have died.

She was thankful he hadn't been with them. All Brian could associate with what happened was that his parents had left without him and had never come back.

There was no use trying to discuss it here. If he brought up staying with Aunt Betty again later, Teresa would talk with him about it.

Her cell phone rang, and she looked at the number before she answered. "Hi, Betty. How is he?" She wrapped an arm around Brian as she listened to Betty talk. "They're doing it tomorrow? Do you need anything?"

"Can I talk to Aunt Betty?"

"Hold on, Brian."

"Tell Rich not to worry about it. I'll make some phone calls tonight." Teresa nodded as she listened. "All right. Brian wants to talk to you."

She handed the phone to him and picked up her slice of pizza.

"How is he?" Maddy asked, as she leaned forward.

"He's resting. They're going to do a procedure tomorrow to open up one of the vessels around the heart."

"How long will he be in the hospital?" Maddy asked as she continued to eat.

"It sounds like he could be home in a day or two if everything goes well. I'll call a couple of guys to help me finish the roof tomorrow."

"Teresa, if you'd rather be at the hospital tomorrow, I understand. Besides, how much are you really going to be able to do with your ankle the way it is?"

"We can't afford to fall any further behind. It'll affect too many other things that have to get done, or we'll blow the schedule." Teresa glanced at her watch. "Wow, eight o'clock. When Brian's done talking with Betty, let's ask for the check. We can have them wrap this if you don't mind. I need to get him home."

By the time they reached Maddy's house, Brian was asleep in the back of the car. After Maddy turned the engine off, both women got out of their seats and walked around to the rear of the Volkswagen.

Teresa balanced on her crutches and slipped her hands through Maddy's thick hair. She leaned in slowly, and kissed her, gentle and quiet-like, until the warmth flickered and Maddy pressed against her.

Maddy could feel the gentle swell of Teresa's breasts and the fullness of her hips as her hands skimmed over the curves of Teresa's body, and she wanted to feel more of that. A moan escaped her lips, and Teresa pulled back slowly.

"It feels so good to kiss you," Teresa said, running her lips across Maddy's face.

Maddy kept her arms wrapped around Teresa's waist. "I can't

argue with that."

"I have to ask you something."

"Uh-oh." Maddy let out a breath.

"I remember what you said the other night about not being used to this. What did you mean?"

"Why are you asking me that?"

"Because I want to know what you meant."

Teresa felt Maddy's hold loosen around her waist.

"I like spending time with you, Teresa. I just...I know we've both been hurt, and it's hard to trust how this feels."

"Part of me," Teresa said, "wants to just jump in feet first, but there's a part of me that can't do that. I'm afraid...now, I sound stupid...but I don't want to get hurt. I know I will at some point, but I don't want Brian to get hurt is more the point. I guess what I'm trying to say is that I want to make sure we're on the same wavelength."

"You don't sound stupid. You sound sincere and honest. I'm pretty sure we're both on the same wavelength. I'm willing to see where this takes us — no rush, no pressure."

Teresa was grateful for Maddy's forthright manner. She considered that an important trait in a friend. She was pretty sure they were friends, but she was less confident of where the feelings she had for Maddy would lead them.

"What are you doing Saturday night?" Teresa said.

"I guess that depends on what you're asking for."

"Because this..." Teresa leaned forward and pressed her lips to Maddy's. This time the heat was already there, and Teresa couldn't get enough of Maddy's mouth. She liked the way their bodies fit together, and the way Maddy's breasts felt in her hands. When she pulled away, they were both breathless. "This makes me want more."

Maddy moved closer, cupping Teresa's face with her hand. "Then the answer is whatever *you* want to do," she said, savoring the moment and thoroughly enjoying Teresa.

"How about dinner at my place? Say seven o'clock? Brian's spending the night with one of his friends."

"I like the sound of that."

"Mmm." A quirky grin curved up a corner of Teresa's mouth. She could get lost in Maddy's eyes and forget about the events of the day for a moment. She took a step back. "I should wake Brian."

"Duty calls, and tomorrow's a school day."

"That sounds almost like something Brian would say. Do you count down the days until school's out, too?" Teresa teased her.

Maddy laughed and jabbed Teresa with her elbow. "Just like the kids."

Chapter
Ten

MADDY OPENED THE door to her apartment and gave her sister a sheepish grin. She had muddled through the week until Thursday, when she called Angela and left a message insisting that she come over as soon as she could.

"Dear God, what happened? It sounded like life or death." Angela walked past Maddy and tossed her purse onto the couch.

"I'm okay." Maddy ran her hands through her hair. "Actually, I'm a nervous wreck."

"Why? What's the matter?"

"Do you remember the weekend we went to the animal shelter benefit and ended up at the baseball field with Teresa and Brian?"

"Yeah, the aunt and the nephew. I remember. What about it?"

"Teresa asked me to come over for dinner Saturday night."

"You're telling me I drove like a bat out of hell for that? I'm happy for you, but for Chrissakes, Maddy, I thought something dreadful happened."

Maddy's expression turned into a pout. "Angela, who else do I have to talk to about the first date I've had since I broke up with Christine?"

"Sorry, b...but wait, a date? And you didn't tell me? You little...I want details." Angela grabbed Maddy's arm and turned her around.

"Details? What do you mean, details?" Maddy easily shook off Angela's grip.

"How did it go from playing baseball with the kid to dinner at the aunt's house? I want those kinds of details. Hey, do you have Pepsi?"

"Yes, yes, I'll get it." Maddy walked into the kitchen and returned a few minutes later with an ice-cold glass of Angela's favorite soft drink.

"So, tell me what happened." Angela sat on the sofa and took a sip of her Pepsi.

"It started with Teresa helping me fix the barn door."

Maddy had thought back to that day so many times she could imagine Teresa sitting across from her at the kitchen table. Something about the way Teresa looked at her had ignited a feeling within Maddy that she couldn't put into words.

"The barn door? Okay, I'm lost. *What* are you talking about?"

"She helped me fix the barn door in return for tutoring Brian."

"I am totally confused." Angela set her glass down on the table and stared at Maddy. "Is this some kind of lesbian mating ritual I don't know about?"

"You are such a pain in the ass, Angela."

Angela winked at Maddy and picked her glass up. "Yes, I know I am. How does she know about fixing doors?"

"She's a carpenter. Actually, she's been doing a lot of the work on my house."

"The house...and you never said anything to me."

"Hey, let go." Maddy pried Angela's gripping fingers from around her knee.

"She's been working here since June, and you didn't tell me?"

"I didn't even know she was Brian's aunt until September."

"Okay, I'll give you that." Angela sat back. "She's very cute. No, not cute. Attractive. Yeah, there's definitely something captivating about those eyes."

"Who knew you paid that much attention that day?"

"I noticed your interest was piqued. Your whole demeanor changed when you saw that woman." Angela smirked. "Don't change the subject, Maddy."

"We both got invited to a cookout last weekend." Maddy felt her face flush. "I stayed to watch some fireworks with Teresa. Brian went out in a boat with Betty, and Teresa and I sat on a swing by the dock."

"Well?" Angela tucked one leg underneath her and leaned forward.

"We talked a little bit, and I was just enjoying spending time with her," Maddy finally said softly, remembering the soft lapping of the water, the cool night air, and the shiver of anticipation she had felt when Teresa turned and looked at her.

"And?" Angela waited a second and then waved her hand in front of Maddy's eyes.

"She kissed me."

"So?" Angela nudged Maddy with her hand. "Is she a good kisser?"

"Angela!"

"You're turning six shades of red, so I'll take that as a yes."

Maddy hid her face in her hands. "You are such a dog."

"I've lived with Tom for ten years. What do you want? I'm

happy for you, Maddy. I hope this turns out to be good for you."

"Thanks." Maddy recovered her composure. "I'm a nervous wreck about seeing her."

"Why?"

"I don't know. She seems special. I haven't been able to put my finger on it, but it's as if something is driving me to her. God, I don't think I'm ready for anything serious like falling in love."

"Love? Who's talking about love? Lighten up and enjoy the evening. It's just dinner."

"I know. I just haven't felt this way in a long time."

"Do yourself a favor, Maddy. Don't go into this with any expectations. Hell, you may find out you don't want to see her again after one date."

"Mmm, I'm not sure that would happen." Maddy watched as Angela finished her drink, carried her glass into the kitchen, and returned.

"I don't think so, either. Just have fun."

"Thanks for coming over, Angie."

"That's what older sisters are for. Right?" Angela retrieved her purse.

Maddy gave her a hug and Angela left. Maddy nibbled her lower lip while she watched the car's taillights recede into the darkness.

No expectations. She didn't have them, really. Her life was neat and ordered. She had been living her own way and handling her own affairs for some time, and she was not about to give that up for just anybody.

IT HAD BEEN a long, exhausting week of work for Teresa. In the end, she was satisfied that none of the projects she and Rich were involved in had suffered any significant setbacks in their respective schedules.

That alone made her feel proud of the effort she'd put in and relieved some of the anxiety she was feeling about her date with Maddy tonight.

She set that thought aside and finished vacuuming the living room. As she dragged the vacuum to the hall closet, she heard Brian calling her from outside.

She maneuvered the upright into the closet and shut the door just as he ran into the house.

"Aunt Teresa. You have to come see this."

"See what?"

"There's a dog down by the creek. It's hurt."

"You didn't get close to it, did you?"

"No, I just saw it when I was throwing rocks."

"I thought we agreed you weren't going to throw rocks since people walk on the bike trails on the other side of the creek." Teresa moved toward the door and guided Brian ahead of her.

"I was just skipping them across the water."

"Well, let's go. I'm not sure what we'll be able to do for it." Teresa hoped that whatever Brian saw had moved on. She wasn't relishing the thought of having to deal with an injured animal. If she was lucky, maybe it would have tags, and she could call the owner to come pick it up.

"It's over here." Brian ran down the gently sloping backyard toward the line of swamp maples that ran along the creek bed.

Teresa tried to jog after him but settled on limping along as quickly as she could. If the animal was frightened, it might bite, and she didn't want Brian to get too near it. When she got closer to where he was pointing, she saw burnt orange fur, and when she squatted down only a couple of feet away, she realized the animal lying on the ground was a red fox.

The only red fox Teresa had seen before was one that trotted nimbly across her path in Loantaka Park a couple of years ago. It carried a Canada goose in its mouth and looked quite pleased with its catch as it disappeared into the brush. Teresa remembered standing there in shock at having seen the sprite little animal.

"He's hurt, Aunt T."

She heard the slight crack of emotion in Brian's voice and reached out to move him back a step. "I know, Brian."

She walked around the animal and peered closely at it. Its eyes were closed, and when she looked at its flank, there was no rise and fall to indicate that it was breathing. She glanced over at Brian and saw his eyes brimming with tears.

"Can you help him?"

"I'm sorry. I think he's already dead."

"Why? What happened to him?"

"Maybe he was sick."

"We can't leave him here like this, Aunt Teresa. He's all alone."

"Brian, we don't have a lot of time. Steve's dad is going to be here soon to pick you up. What do you want to do?"

"Can we cover him?"

Teresa looked around at the rocks along the edge of the creek bed and decided if covering the fox would make Brian feel better, then it was worth doing. She could call animal control later to pick up the carcass.

"Brian, get one of the old bath towels out of the cabinet in the laundry room. Bring it back here."

While he was gone, Teresa began gathering rocks. She had accumulated a fair-sized pile by the time he returned. He crouched on his heels and stared sadly at the dead animal.

"Hand me the towel." She shook the old blue towel out and draped it over the fox's limp form.

"All right, start setting the rocks around the edges to hold the towel down. Try not to touch the blanket too much."

This was not how she had planned to spend the afternoon, but she sensed it was important to Brian to do this. Teresa was touched by how gently Brian set the rocks in place around the fox. He went about his task somberly, and they had positioned a small circle of rocks around the body when they were finished.

"He'll be safe there tonight. I'll call someone tomorrow, so they can pick him up."

"What will happen to him?"

Teresa chose her words carefully. "They'll give him a proper burial, Brian."

"Will he be alone?"

"He won't be alone in heaven."

Brian stared down at the rocks and then looked back at Teresa. "Is this what happened to Mommy and Daddy when they died?"

Teresa reached over to pull him close to her. "When we die, we go to heaven."

"Does it hurt?"

Teresa hadn't anticipated the questions that this animal's death provoked in Brian, and her heart quickened as she formed her answer. "We don't need our bodies anymore when we go to heaven."

"But if Mommy and Daddy don't need their bodies, how will I find them when *I* get there?" Tears slipped down Brian's cheeks, and he licked them off his lips.

Teresa got down on one knee and rubbed his arms. "People don't change when they get to heaven. Everyone looks just the way you remember them looking here on earth."

"I still love them."

"Of course you do." She pulled him into a hug. "We don't stop loving people when they die. We miss them terribly, but we never stop loving them."

Teresa lifted her head at the honking of a horn. "I think your ride is here." She wiped tears from her eyes and took a deep breath. "Are you okay?"

Brian rubbed his eyes and nodded. "I'm okay."

"Come on." Teresa held out her hand, and together they walked up to the house.

"Brian!" Steven ran around the corner of the house and

stopped short when he saw them.

Steven's father rounded the corner a moment later. "Everything all right?" he asked.

Teresa tipped her head to look up at Mike. He was a tall, burly man with a smile that lit up his face. She had done work remodeling a bathroom for his home last year. With the two boys in the same grade at school, the two families had quickly become friends. "Brian found a red fox down by the creek. He must have been sick."

"Do you want to see what we did, Steven?" Brian asked.

"Yeah."

"Come on. I'll show you." The boys raced off down the hill to the creek.

"We covered him with a bath towel. Do you think animal control will pick him up if I call them?"

"One of my buddies knows the supervisor, so let me know if there's a problem. Is Brian okay?"

"It brought up some questions about death and heaven."

Mike shook his head. "I don't know how you handle it."

"On a wing and prayer is what it feels like."

"Come on, guys," Mike called out. "The movie starts in a half hour."

"Brian," Teresa said, "your bag's on the couch. I'll meet you around front. Make sure you wash your hands before you leave."

"Okay." Brian raced past Teresa with Steven close on his heels.

"I'll be home, Mike, if you need to get hold of me," Teresa said, as they walked around to the front yard.

"Don't worry about it. I'm sure he'll be fine."

A couple of minutes later, the two boys burst through the front door and ran over to where Teresa and Mike were standing. "Have fun, Brian. Make sure you do what the Connors tell you to do."

"I will."

Teresa gave Brian a hug and waved as he climbed into the Subaru wagon. She checked her watch as they drove off. She had two hours to finish up with the house and get ready before Maddy arrived.

Chapter
Eleven

IN THE SHOWER, inhaling a fresh lavender smell, Teresa had rinsed herself clean from the day. After dressing in jeans and a peach-colored T-shirt, she hurried around and straightened up a bit. She rearranged the knick-knacks on a bookshelf and checked on the steaks marinating in the refrigerator.

As she washed lettuce and sliced raw vegetables for the salad, her thoughts strayed, and she considered how little she knew about Maddy. She had known what to expect with Erin, her likes and dislikes, her moods, and that she didn't like to talk until after she had her first cup of coffee in the morning.

Here she was at forty, thinking about starting over again.

She was tossing everything together in a large bowl when she heard the doorbell ring. She felt a nervous flutter in her belly.

"I'm coming." She wiped her hands on a dishtowel and walked out of the kitchen.

When she reached the door and opened it, Maddy greeted her with a charming smile.

"I picked up a bottle of red wine to go with dinner," Maddy said, her eyes going over Teresa. "That's a great color on you."

"Thanks. You look nice, too. Come on in." Maddy's hair was still damp from the shower, and she looked relaxed as she walked past Teresa in a pair of blue jeans, loafers, and a white shirt.

"The wine was a great idea. I have steaks marinating in the refrigerator." Teresa led the way to the kitchen.

"You're not using your crutches?"

"The swelling went down, and it doesn't hurt much anymore."

"Can I help with anything?" Maddy set the bottle on the counter and gave an appreciative glance at the salad. "That looks delicious."

Teresa was acutely aware of the effect Maddy's closeness was having on her, and she found it difficult to pay attention to what she was doing. "Sit. Relax. I'll pour us some wine."

Maddy sat in the kitchen chair. Teresa pulled the wineglasses

out of a cabinet and uncorked the wine. It gave Maddy the
opportunity to soak in the back view of Teresa with her softly
curved hips, broad shoulders, and the exposed nape of her neck.

"Were the directions okay?"

Maddy took a second to pull her wayward thoughts together.
"They were perfect, considering I live barely ten minutes from
you."

Teresa laughed as she poured the wine.

"What's funny?" Maddy leaned forward, wondering as she did
if that really was a flush of color she saw on Teresa's cheeks.

"I think I'm actually nervous and saying that makes me feel
silly."

"You're just being honest. I like that." A smile tugged at
Maddy's lips as she stood up and stepped closer. She took the
glasses out of Teresa's hands and set them on the counter. "Maybe
this will help."

Maddy touched two fingers under Teresa's chin, leaned in
slowly, and kissed her gently until the touch sparked little flashes
of heat deep down inside.

Through the tentative touch of her lips, Maddy was smiling
and Teresa smiled a little, too, as she slid her hands over Maddy's
shoulders.

Maddy subtly increased the pressure of each stroke of her
tongue until Teresa's lips parted beneath hers. The kiss turned hot
and deliberately seductive. Maddy watched Teresa through the kiss
and saw her hazel eyes darken with barely veiled desire.

When she stepped back, Maddy lifted the wineglasses and
gave one to Teresa. "Do you have any idea how good it felt to kiss
you just now?"

Teresa blushed and took a sip of her wine to calm her racing
pulse. She was having a hard time believing how one simple kiss
had left her with such lustful desire. "You have very kissable lips."

"We could start again."

"Oh, God." Teresa laughed and wrapped an arm around
Maddy's neck. "We'll never eat."

"Mmm, you have a point," Maddy teased, as Teresa released
her and stepped away.

"I should light the grill. Care to join me outside?"

"Yes. Are you sure there's nothing I can help you with?"

"You can take the steaks out of the refrigerator. By the time the
grill's hot, they'll be ready to go on."

Maddy opened the refrigerator door, pulled out the platter of
steaks, and set them on the counter. The screen door closed behind
her, and she heard Teresa outside. Maddy let her head fall forward
and drew a long, steadying breath to regain her equilibrium. She

smoothed her shirt, picked up her wineglass, and stepped outside.

She gazed at the gently sloping backyard that ended where a wooded area began. She heard birds chattering and small woodland creatures scampering through the underbrush. Teresa was standing by the grill staring out at the woods as if lost in thought.

"This is beautiful back here, so peaceful."

"The Great Swamp starts about fifty feet away from that creek back there."

"Really?" Maddy sipped her wine. "You must get to see a lot of animals."

Teresa checked the burners on the gas grill and then closed the lid. "We get our fair share of wildlife meandering through the yard. I'm going to screen in this porch next spring. In the summer, you can't sit out here with the mosquitoes."

Maddy walked up and stood beside Teresa. "How's Rich doing?"

"He's taking it easy for now. He has to make changes, eat healthier foods, and exercise."

"I hope he takes care of himself."

"I hope so, too." Teresa offered Maddy her hand. She led her over to the porch, and they sat together on the first step.

"Where's Brian tonight?"

"Over at a friend's house. Steven's father picked him up about two hours ago. They were kicking the night off with a movie."

"He must have been excited."

"That's all I heard about all week long." Teresa gave Maddy a sidelong glance. "You'd think it would be a welcome relief to have an entire night to myself, but there's a part of me that misses him."

"You deserve a break every now and then. I can't imagine myself raising a child alone."

Teresa huffed out a sigh. "There are days when it's the hardest thing I've ever done."

"I imagine it can be. So tell me about yourself, Teresa."

"You know my story."

"I only know part of it. Tell me about your family."

"Let me get the steaks on first." Teresa stood up, climbed the steps, and lifted the platter of steaks from the kitchen counter.

Maddy reached out and affectionately touched the back of Teresa's leg when she passed her on the way to the grill. There was a loud sizzle as Teresa placed each steak on the grates.

She sat back down beside Maddy. "How do you like your steak cooked?"

"Medium, please. You were going to tell me about your family."

"Right." Teresa rubbed her palms across her thighs. "Well, out of the four of us, David was the only one I was willing to spend a lot of my time with when I was growing up. We were always close, and he was a good listener. That was one of his best qualities. My mother and father were too caught up in their own issues to really listen to anything we had to say. They would sit, but you could tell they weren't hearing what you said. They hardly heard each other most of the time. Whenever I needed to talk, David was always there for me. He was my mother's favorite child. When she buried him, part of her went with him. After that, she was never the same."

Maddy blinked back tears. "That's so sad. Parents aren't supposed to bury their children."

"No, they're not." Teresa took a sip of her wine and glanced up at the dark thunderheads that were gathering in the distant sky above the trees. "It looks like we may get a storm."

"I thought I heard something about a chance of rain tonight."

"If we're lucky, the steaks will get done out here. If not, I'll stick them under the broiler when we go inside. Anyway," Teresa said, after she collected her thoughts, "my father, Robert Parker, was a jerk. He was never that way to David and me, but he was a jerk toward my mom. He left her, and she had to work two jobs to put food on the table and pay the mortgage. Looking back, I think she loved him, but I don't know whether my father was ever emotionally capable of loving anyone."

The wind started to kick up, and the branches in the tops of the trees started to rustle. Teresa stood up and walked over to the grill. She lifted the edges of the steaks with a pair of tongs and flipped them over. She closed the lid of the grill, walked back to Maddy, and resumed her story.

"David swore he would do everything in his power not to be like our father, and he did. What's not fair is that some stinking drunken driver killed David and Fran before they had the chance to see their son grow up."

Maddy put her arm around Teresa's shoulder, leaned in, and brushed her lips against Teresa's temple in a gesture of comfort. "I'm sorry you lost your brother."

"You know why I worry about Brian so much? I worry that he's going to live his life being afraid to love someone because if he does, they'll either die first or leave him."

"I can understand that." Maddy met Teresa's gaze and said with quiet sincerity. "But people do die and sometimes they leave us. That's the way life is. All you can do is give him a strong foundation, love him, and be there for him. The rest is up to him."

They both looked up as the plops of big, fat raindrops

splattered the ground around them.

"Uh-oh." Teresa jumped to her feet and ran to the grill. She quickly removed the steaks and turned off the gas. By the time she made it back to the porch, the skies had opened up, and the rain was pouring down.

Maddy took the platter from her. "You got soaked. Grab the wineglasses and go change your shirt. I'll turn the broiler on."

"Thanks." Teresa led the way inside, set the wineglasses on the counter, and disappeared into the bedroom. She stripped off her wet shirt and bra, trading them for a gray pullover sweatshirt.

Maddy had the broiler turned on when Teresa returned, and she set the steaks underneath the flame.

"It'll be quick. Two minutes," she said, as she pulled out a couple of plates and handed them to Maddy. "Put those on the table."

"Where do you keep your utensils?"

"In the drawer to my right."

Maddy set out forks and knives. "Can I pour you more wine?"

"That would be great. Thanks."

Teresa pulled a container of salad dressing out of the refrigerator and drizzled some over the salad. She opened the oven door, grabbed an oven mitt, and after a moment, removed the steaks. "Okay, we're ready."

WHILE THEY ATE, the rain fell steadily and lightning lit up the sky, followed by the occasional rumble of thunder. Teresa reached for the bottle of wine. She topped off her glass and held it up, eyebrows raised to Maddy.

"Yes, thanks. I love a good thunderstorm." Maddy cut a piece of steak and popped it into her mouth. She chewed thoughtfully and swallowed. "This is delicious."

"It's just olive oil, fresh garlic, thyme, a good sprinkling of cracked black peppercorns, and some sea salt."

"I love it."

They chatted amiably about Brian, the school, and the work that Teresa was doing on Maddy's new house. The conversation faded as they continued to eat.

Maddy finished her salad and took a sip of her wine. "How did you get involved in the construction business?"

"After the accident, I quit my job at the accounting firm I worked for. I just couldn't do it anymore. Rich had always joked about us working together, so I called him one day and asked him if he was serious about it. He was and the rest is history."

"Did you know Rich before that?"

"We grew up together. I had helped him before on small jobs when he was first starting out. It's better than sitting behind a desk manipulating spreadsheets and getting creative with tax loopholes."

"Changing careers like that took a lot of guts." Maddy stood up. "I'll take care of the plates."

"You don't have to," Teresa said as she carried her dish to the sink.

"Uh-uh. You cooked. It's only fair."

Giving in, Teresa walked into the living room and lit a couple of candles. She was thumbing through her CD collection when Maddy joined her a few minutes later. "Any requests?"

Maddy peered at the choices. She selected one. "How's this?"

"Enya. Perfect." Teresa slipped the CD into the player, and a moment later, the haunting melody of cellos filled the air. She adjusted the volume and walked over to sit on the couch. She patted the cushion next to her.

Maddy sat beside her. She felt drawn to so much about Teresa, especially her quiet self-reliance. Relaxing, she settled against Teresa's body.

The warmth of the contact between them heated Teresa's blood and her heart beat faster. "I can't remember the last time I just sat and listened to music like this."

Maddy shifted and looked at Teresa. She slid an arm across and rested her hand on Teresa's stomach. She gently kneaded the sweatshirt's soft fabric between her fingers. "It's nice to be able to share it with someone."

Maddy felt the tremor that went through Teresa, and she leaned closer, her lips lightly brushing Teresa's at first and then more ardently as a soft moan escaped Teresa's throat. She raised the bottom of Teresa's sweatshirt and slipped her hand underneath to caress the soft skin.

Teresa felt the fire rush through her blood, and all the needs and fantasies coalesced in the blind heat of desire. The taste of Maddy's tongue, the caressing touch that explored her skin, cupped her breasts, and hardened her nipples stoked passions that she had long denied.

"Maddy," Teresa murmured when Maddy lifted her mouth and brushed her lips back and forth in a light, teasing kiss.

"Yes?"

"Dear God, don't stop."

"I wouldn't think of it."

Maddy couldn't get enough of Teresa, her mouth, her throat, her breasts. The gasps and moans and soft cries of pleasure fired her passions, and she shuddered as a flood of moist heat gushed between her thighs.

Teresa growled as the button and zipper on Maddy's jeans slowed her exploration.

"Here." Maddy stood up, kicked off her loafers, and wriggled out of her jeans.

Teresa breathed heavily as she gazed up the length of Maddy's partially clothed body. She stood and kissed her again, gently this time, as her fingers worked the buttons loose on Maddy's shirt.

When she was finished, Maddy stood in front of her in a white lacy bra and panties. Teresa pulled the straps down with her thumbs and let them hang loose on Maddy's arms. She cupped Maddy's breasts and kissed each one tenderly before sliding her hands around Maddy's back and unhooking her bra. She pulled the bra away from her breasts and let it fall to the floor.

Teresa's warm mouth touched Maddy's in a slow exploration of her full lips before she moved upward over Maddy's flushed cheek. She kissed each eyelid and then worked her way down along Maddy's jawline, to find her mouth again.

"You're beautiful, Maddy."

Maddy blushed at the compliment and nuzzled Teresa's neck. She loosened Teresa's belt and undid the button and zipper of her jeans while Teresa continued to run her hands over Maddy's shoulders and neck.

They both laughed a moment later as Teresa fought with the laces on her sneakers and plopped unceremoniously on the couch as she lost her balance.

When Teresa stepped out of her jeans and shed her panties, Maddy's gaze drifted boldly over her body, studying her breasts and belly, then down to the curly hair between her thighs. Maddy reached out and settled her hands on Teresa's waist. She trailed her hands up and cupped Teresa's breasts, savoring the soft intake of breath when she brushed a nipple with her thumb. She closed her eyes with pleasure at the sensation of Teresa's nipples hardening beneath her touch. Maddy lowered her head and captured a nipple between her lips, suckling gently. She increased the pressure until she heard Teresa's first gasp of pleasure.

Teresa tugged Maddy down to her, and they lay in a tangle of warm limbs. Teresa ran her hand up the inside of Maddy's thigh, caressing and teasing as Maddy's lovely hips lifted to her touch.

Teresa bit her lip to hide her smile as she tugged Maddy's panties down and tossed them to the floor. She stroked her fingers through the triangle of hair and took great pleasure in finding the silky wetness already covering her lips. Teresa nudged her fingers inside of Maddy and started a slow, teasing motion with her hand while she watched Maddy look back at her with desire.

Teresa's touch drove Maddy wild, and she arched and twisted, her body begging to feel Teresa fill her completely. Maddy found Teresa's mouth, and her hands stroked over Teresa's breasts.

Teresa trailed her fingertips over Maddy's skin, her electrifying touch lighting little fires, and she finally clasped Maddy's wandering hands, pulling them away before they aroused her too quickly.

Maddy gasped when Teresa slid two fingers slowly inside, filling her as she circled another over her clitoris.

Together, they found a rhythm. Teresa slowed her movements as she felt Maddy shudder and tighten her grip on her shoulders.

"Please. Don't stop."

She found a spot that made Maddy cry out and push against her hand, forcing Teresa deeper into her. Teresa felt the walls of Maddy's vagina spasm and contract, and she pulled back, deliberately wanting to prolong her orgasm.

"Please…"

Maddy wrapped her legs around Teresa's hips and pulled the full length of her fingers into her arching body. Teresa drove her fingers into Maddy with long, deep, slow strokes. Maddy buried her face in the curve of Teresa's neck. Her body shuddered and Maddy cried out in mindless pleasure, clutching at Teresa's sweat-slicked skin as an orgasm rolled through her.

SOMETIME LATER, TERESA led Maddy into her bedroom, and they climbed under the covers and snuggled together in the warm afterglow. Teresa stretched, and Maddy propped herself up on one elbow.

She ran her fingertips over Teresa's belly and traced them over the small scar that ran across Teresa's lower abdomen.

"What happened here?"

Teresa lifted her head for a quick glance. "I had appendicitis when I was a kid."

Maddy lowered her head onto Teresa's chest. She could hear the murmur of Teresa's heartbeat coupled with the thrumming of the rain on the roof. Outside, a flash of lightning lit up the room and thunder rumbled menacingly overhead.

"It's been so long, I think I forgot how good this could feel."

Teresa chuckled softly. "Your body surely didn't forget."

"I haven't been with anyone since I broke up with Christine."

Teresa was quiet for a moment as she considered how to respond. "It can be good to be alone after a breakup. You get to find out who you are again on your own terms."

"Was it that way for you?"

"No. I was in a fog after the accident. I knew things weren't right between Erin and me. I came home one day after work, and she started on me. She said I had emotionally deserted her. She was tired of taking a backseat to Brian's needs and my work."

"What did she expect?"

"She was right, Maddy."

"What did she think was going to happen after you lost your brother and took in Brian?"

"I don't know, but it wasn't what she wanted."

"So, she just walked out?"

"She said goodbye to Brian one morning before school and packed her bags while we were gone. I think her leaving hurt him more than it hurt me. The look on his face when he realized she'd left just tore me up inside."

"What did you do?"

"What I had to do. I just kept building one project after another. I worked, paid the bills, Brian went to school, and another year went by. This spring came, and I saw the buds form on the trees while we laid the foundation for your house. I smelled the rain and the grass and heard the birds singing for the first time in a long while."

"It sounds as though the fog was starting to lift."

Teresa saw the faint smile on Maddy's face and realized she understood what she meant.

"I met you, and here we are."

"Shh." Maddy put her fingers over Teresa's lips. "Just be here with me right now."

Maddy trailed her hand down Teresa's belly while she leaned over and captured a nipple between her lips. She heard Teresa groan when her fingers teased and caressed the silkiness between Teresa's thighs. Her lips roamed over Teresa's body. Maddy stroked her tongue over her flesh and into her dewy softness, driving Teresa wild.

Teresa's hips rocked and bucked of their own volition as her body went hot from her head to her toes, and she came hard. She was desperate for more, and Maddy filled her, taking her quickly over the edge again until her body went limp. Teresa heard herself moan, and she clung desperately to Maddy, wanting to remember every second and every moment of their magical time together.

They made love several more times that night and fell asleep in each other's arms just after two in the morning.

Maddy woke as darkness was giving way to the first hues of light on the horizon. Teresa traced her fingers down the smooth skin of Maddy's abdomen and then rolled over on top of her. Maddy's auburn curls were in disarray, her cheeks and the tops of her breasts were still flushed from their lovemaking, but her eyes flared with a sultry desire as Teresa covered her mouth with her soft lips.

The intense urgency of their earlier lovemaking was replaced with a slow, passionate sensuality. Teresa drove Maddy to climax, whispering words of encouragement that were as erotic and arousing to Maddy as the sensual touch of her lover's hands. Maddy's hips matched the rhythm of Teresa's thrusting hand, and she frantically begged, "Please," repeatedly.

After the last shudders of pleasure began to ebb, Teresa cradled Maddy close to her body and buried her face in the curve of Maddy's neck. They lay in bed, watching through the window as the sun rose over the horizon and brightened the dense leafy tops of the trees. Neither spoke and Maddy sensed that their lovemaking had been a profound, almost spiritual experience for both of them.

TERESA HAD HER first cup of coffee with Maddy as they made breakfast. They sat at the kitchen table and ate fried eggs with bacon and toast.

"What do you have to do today?" Teresa asked in between bites.

"I've got lesson plans to review, and I'm raising a collection of basic necessities to help hurricane victims. The class is in charge of sorting through what we collect so it can be packaged and shipped out."

"That's a great project."

"It's a good way for the kids to feel they can help, and they start to develop a sense that life is greater than just themselves."

"I think that's fantastic." Teresa found it admirable that Maddy felt strongly about instilling values like that in her students.

After they cleaned up the kitchen, they took a walk along the edge of the creek.

"What's that?" Maddy pointed to the blue blanket that was covering the fox.

Teresa sighed. "Brian discovered a fox that had died yesterday. I have to call animal control to come pick it up."

"Did it upset him?"

"Yeah, it did. His questions get harder to answer. 'Did it hurt when Mom and Dad died? How will I know them when I get to heaven?' It makes me ache in the pit of my stomach."

Teresa was surprised to see tears in Maddy's eyes when she looked at her. She offered a sad smile of acknowledgement as she wiped away the tear that rolled down Maddy's cheek.

"Sometimes it used to feel like David and Fran were just away on a long vacation." Teresa took Maddy's hand as they walked back to the house.

Teresa didn't want Maddy to leave. At the same time, she didn't think Brian needed to know that Maddy had spent the night.

Teresa made no plans with Maddy for later. They both decided to see what the week brought with their respective schedules. Teresa thought that was just as well. She needed time to think about what direction they might be taking.

She grabbed her second cup of coffee after she called animal control and was on her way to pick up Brian from Steven's house.

He was quiet on the ride home, and she chalked it up to the boys probably staying up late. The quiet gave her time to think.

She didn't have much experience with long-term relationships outside of Erin. She hoped that last night was more than just a fling. She thought it was more, but how would she know if this was real? What would she say to Brian? And what would he think about it?

Unfamiliar emotions filled her heart. She decided it was better to drink her coffee and watch Brian launch a wooden plane into the air than to dwell on whether she and Maddy were meant to be together. The toy looped once high up in the air and glided softly back down to the earth not far from where Brian was standing.

He had been subdued and almost pensive since she picked him up earlier. Something was bothering him.

"Are you hungry, Brian?"

He picked up his plane, adjusted the wings, and then glanced back at where she was sitting. "A little."

"I'll throw some burgers on the grill." Teresa went inside. She was just pulling out a package of hamburger meat when the screen door opened and closed.

"Aunt Teresa?"

She looked at Brian and felt a surge of emotion. His little boy face was changing so fast from week to week. "What is it?"

"What does it mean when you get to first base?"

There was a thud as the package of meat slipped through her fingers and fell to the floor. "First base..." Teresa's mind raced furiously through an image of baseball and landed squarely on an image of what she could not believe just came out of her six-year-old nephew's mouth.

She had an idea of where the question came from. Steven had an older brother who was in eighth grade. The stories she heard about what kids knew about sex and actually did nowadays made her shudder with a dread of what was to come. "Brian," she said as she bent and picked up the package of meat. Brian was still rooted in the same spot. "If it's what they called it when I was your age, it's a kiss on the mouth."

"Oh." He frowned and shifted his feet. "Kenny said that's what people do when they go out together."

"Steven's older brother?"

"Yeah."

Teresa felt like she was about to freefall off a cliff as she prepared herself to ask the next question. "Is there anything else you want to ask me?"

"No."

Thank God!

"Well, is Ms. Geddes going to live with us like Aunt Erin did?"

Oh, boy. Teresa exhaled. "I knew Erin for a long time. I've only known Ms. Geddes for a month."

"But maybe she will?"

"I don't know. People don't just meet and decide they want to live together. It takes time for people to figure out whether that's the right thing for them to do. Why do you ask?"

"She's a nice lady. I like her."

"She is a nice person."

"Do we have potato chips?"

Teresa marveled at how quickly Brian could flit from one subject to another without missing a beat. "In the cabinet." He pulled the bag out and walked outside. Teresa tilted her neck and looked up at the ceiling.

"Somehow, David, I know you're up there laughing at me right now."

Chapter
Twelve

ON WEDNESDAY, TERESA stopped at the school to pick up Brian. She arrived just as the dismissal bell rang and witnessed the organized chaos of students and schoolteachers exiting the building. She sat in her truck for a moment and absorbed the chorus of excited young voices and the rush of activity as teachers made sure that all the kids got on the right buses or to the person who was picking them up.

She noticed the black BMW that pulled into the parking lot and rolled to a stop far away from the bustling activity. Her curiosity piqued as Christine Stewart stepped out of the sports car.

Teresa's eyes narrowed, and she felt an ugly surge of jealousy well up inside her. There was only one reason that she could think of why Christine had come to the school. She had come to see Maddy.

Christine walked out of sight around the corner of the school building. Teresa climbed out of her truck and waited for Brian. Maddy's class would be out shortly.

When the door to the school opened again, Maddy stepped outside and glanced around the parking lot. A smile broke across her features when she spotted Teresa, and she waved to her.

Teresa returned the wave and strode forward across the blacktop. As he walked past several classmates, Brian spotted Teresa and broke into a run.

"Aunt Teresa, look!" He waved a paper as he stopped just shy of her.

"Let me see."

"I wrote a story about going swimming at Uncle Rich's house."

Teresa carefully took the lined paper and read the words. A few were misspelled, but she could see the vast improvement in his work since he began his tutoring sessions with Maddy.

"That's great, Brian. I am so proud of you." With her heart aching, she hugged him tightly.

Maddy walked over to them. "Brian did a very good job

writing that story today."

"I see a difference in just the few weeks since you've been working with him."

"He's the one doing the hard work."

Brian waved his paper over his head. "Do you have any food, Teresa?"

Teresa smiled. "You are a bottomless pit. There's an apple inside the cooler." She ruffled his hair affectionately. "Sit in the truck while I talk to Ms. Geddes."

"Okay."

Maddy waited until Brian was out of earshot, and then turned to Teresa. "I've missed you terribly."

"I think about you all the time." Teresa thrilled with the feeling that Maddy had been as affected by their night of lovemaking as she had been. She wanted to believe that it had been more than just a sexual encounter. She needed to believe it.

"When can I see you again?" Maddy studied Teresa, trying to gauge her expression. Since Saturday, her attraction to Teresa had become something much different from what she had intended. She felt a wild sense of urgency only Teresa could quell.

"Is Saturday okay?"

Maddy had the urge to hook her arms around Teresa's waist. She had been wanting and needing Teresa since they parted on Sunday. "I have to wait that long?"

"During the week is going to be tough to do."

"I know. I'm just teasing you." The expression on Maddy's face froze, and Teresa thought she paled slightly. "Oh, dear."

"What's wrong?" Teresa searched Maddy's features for some sign.

"Christine," she said softly, and then seemed to pull herself together. "That's my ex. She called me a few weeks ago. I guess she finally got the guts to track me down here."

"I'll just...I'll go so you can talk," Teresa managed to say as she nervously rubbed her hands together.

"Teresa, please..." Maddy didn't finish when she realized asking Teresa to stay would be hurtful to both her and Brian.

Teresa tried to keep her demeanor casual. "Brian has an appointment I have to get him to." She lied, not wanting to see Maddy with Christine. "Call me tonight if you want to."

"I will." Torn, Maddy allowed herself one more glance in Teresa's direction before she turned away.

Christine had paused and put her hand to her forehead to shield her eyes from the sun, as she looked toward them. Apparently recognizing Maddy, she walked in her direction.

As Christine approached, Maddy could see that she was

wearing an elegantly tailored business suit and high heels. Her hair was styled just right, her lipstick was unsmudged, and she wore just enough makeup to accent her pale blue eyes.

Teresa heard Christine's voice as she climbed up into the driver's seat of her truck. The rumble of the engine as she turned the key in the ignition drowned out the conversation.

"Madeline, I've been looking all over for you," Christine called out as she glanced toward Teresa's truck. "I looked inside for you, but you weren't in your classroom."

"I always come out with the kids. You know that."

"I love your classroom. It looks so...colorful."

"It's first grade, Christine. The classroom should be cheerful and engaging for the kids."

"I guess it does. I came by your house last week, but you weren't there. The new construction looks impressive."

"Why would you come to my house? You know I teach all day."

"I don't know. Silly mistake, that's all. Who was that woman you were talking to?"

"Her son is in my class."

"You always were dedicated. I was wondering, are you free now? Maybe we can get a cup of coffee."

"I have a meeting in fifteen minutes."

"Well, then walk with me."

Maddy hung her head and then motioned Christine to walk with her.

"I think living out here suits you."

"Really? What makes you say that?" Maddy was shocked at the unexpected compliment.

"You look relaxed...happy."

"I am."

Christine turned and faced Maddy. "Can you honestly look me in the eyes and tell me that there's no chance for us?"

Maddy lifted her head and gazed at Christine for a moment. "Yes, I can."

"I don't believe you. How can you say that, Madeline? After everything that we meant to each other."

"Christine, our relationship had been over a long time before Tina came along. Whatever chance was left for us, you threw away when you slept with her."

"Maddy, it was a mistake. Other people have problems and stay together."

"I'm not other people. I can't trust someone who cheats on me."

"I still love you, Maddy."

"Christine, this conversation is pointless. Please, don't do this."

"We can work this out."

"It's long past the time for working out our problems."

Christine leaned toward Maddy. "That's not what you used to say."

Maddy shot Christine an icy stare. "That was a long time ago, and you don't know me anymore."

"I can't believe you've changed that much since you moved out here."

"Why is that so difficult for you to understand? We are done, we're over. I don't love you anymore."

"How can you be so cruel? I never stopped loving you."

"I'm going to be late for my meeting. Goodbye, Christine." Maddy avoided Christine's outstretched hand and walked into the school building without a backward glance.

By the time she reached the stairs, Maddy was so angry she was shaking and she practically plowed right into Betty.

"Oh! I'm sorry, Betty. I didn't see you."

"I know, dear. You look upset. Is everything all right?"

"Yes, of course. How's Rich doing? I haven't had a chance to see you since you came back to work." Maddy tucked a strand of hair behind her ear.

"I'm just back part time for the next few weeks. Rich can't drive yet, and between his cardiac rehab and doctors' appointments, it's easier for me right now."

"Well, it's good to see you back. Maybe we can grab lunch together soon."

"That'll be nice. I'll see you tomorrow, Maddy." Betty walked away as Maddy hurried up the stairs.

TERESA KEPT HERSELF busy with chores all evening. Brian had been unusually quiet and even went to bed early. For her own part, she tossed and turned as she watched the hours tick by on the clock. She refused to acknowledge that she was upset about Maddy's ex-lover showing up at school.

But Teresa couldn't stop her mind from thinking about them and wondering what they still meant to each other.

She drove herself crazy speculating about what they talked about after she drove away. Did Christine want to get back together with Maddy? How did Maddy feel toward her ex-lover? Teresa was angry with herself for thinking of Maddy in this way, but she couldn't stop her imagination from conjuring up all kinds of scenarios.

When the alarm rang the next morning, she felt as if she had barely slept for a solid hour all night. She dragged herself out of bed and hurried to get Brian ready to meet the school bus.

She spent the next several hours cleaning up some paperwork that Rich would normally do. By the time she got to the work site, clouds had slowly billowed on the horizon. The air was thick with humidity, and the electrician and plumber working inside Maddy's house were hot, sweaty, and irritable.

The mood didn't improve any after Teresa did a walk-through with the plumber and discovered several glaring discrepancies from the master blueprints.

Sam's ears turned red as Teresa unrolled the blueprints on an overturned crate outside the house and pointed out where he needed to make changes. He took out a cigarette and, after lighting it, sucked on it and blew out a puff of smoke.

"Listen, I am not going to pay my guy overtime to reroute those pipes." He jabbed the cigarette at Teresa as he made his point.

"Sam, I'm not arguing with you about this," Teresa said, calmly. "If you don't fix this by the end of business on Thursday, I'll hold up your payment."

"Rich wouldn't do that."

"He wants this job done the right way and on time. The inspection is on Friday. Either fix it, or you're not being paid. Am I making myself clear?"

Sam's face was completely red and his jugular veins bulged. He stuffed the cigarette back into his mouth and stomped off to his truck.

The electrician walked out of the house and gave Teresa a sheepish grin. "Sam's not used to being held accountable, let alone by a woman."

"Ed, you've worked with me before. All I ask is that people do the work right. If they do that, then I don't have a problem with them."

"I know. That's not unreasonable. Listen, all the lines are run, so we're ready for the electrical inspection."

"Great. Thank you. See you later, Ed."

"So long."

Teresa made a note to check the plumbing rerouting on Friday morning. As she folded up the blueprints, large, fat raindrops started falling. She glanced up at the sky and thought about making a dash for her truck, but the rain started to fall in torrents.

"Well, this is a perfect end to a sucky day."

She stepped back inside and decided to wait and see if the rain let up. While rummaging through some leftover supplies in search of a plastic bag, she thought she heard a car drive up.

Teresa walked to the door and was surprised to see Maddy's yellow Volkswagen parked next to her truck. A moment later, the driver's side door opened and Maddy made a dash for the overhang as the rain teemed down. She wrapped Teresa in a wet hug.

"I have pizza in the car."

Teresa tilted her head and gazed into Maddy's eyes as she held Maddy in her arms. She brushed the wet curls back from Maddy's forehead. "Is that a bribe to stay for dinner?"

She heard the rain pummeling the roof and thunder rumbled ominously around them.

"It could be."

"Brian told me he was going to Betty's for dinner, so I called in an order for a large pepperoni pie. I hoped I would catch you here before you left for the day."

"I'm glad you did."

"Come on, we'll make a run for it."

"Hold on. I have to find something to put the blueprints in, or they'll get ruined."

Together they managed to find a garbage bag among the piles of scrap wood and leftover supplies from the different subcontractors. Teresa stuck the blueprints into it, and they made a sloppy dash to the car.

THEY WERE BOTH drenched by the time they made it into Maddy's apartment.

"I'm sorry about Christine showing up yesterday," Maddy said.

"Why? You have nothing to be sorry for," Teresa replied, although hearing the words made her feel more confident of where she stood with Maddy.

"I've tried to be nice and tell her that there's no chance of us getting back together, but she won't give up."

"She seems like a woman who's used to getting what she wants."

"Christine is a corporate lawyer on the fast track, and she lets that intensity carry over into how she conducts her personal life."

"Sounds like she needs to hear it loud and clear in one syllable words." Teresa caught the shuttered look in Maddy's eyes, and then it was gone.

"You must be cold," Maddy said. "Let me get you a dry T-shirt."

"Thanks."

Teresa followed Maddy into her bedroom and accepted the

shirt that Maddy handed her. She couldn't help but inhale the scent of Maddy's perfume as she tugged the shirt over her head.

With Maddy's hair wet and the curls framing her face, Teresa decided she looked intoxicatingly beautiful. "You look very sexy."

"You look sexy enough to take to bed right now."

"Oh, God," Teresa said with a moan. "I have to pick up Brian."

Before Teresa could react, Maddy wrapped her arms around her. She caressed Teresa's lips with hers, squeezed her buttocks, and tugged playfully at her bottom lip at the end of a passionate kiss.

"There." Maddy stepped back and smiled seductively. "You left me wanting and needing you all week. Now it's your turn. Let's go eat pizza."

Maddy turned and walked out of the room but not before Teresa got a squeeze in of her own.

"Just you wait." Teresa caught Maddy from behind and nipped the back of her neck, eliciting a yelp of surprise from her.

"Promises, promises." Maddy slipped away and fended off Teresa's wandering hands.

They ended up in the kitchen, laughing, and embraced in another ardent kiss that left them both a little breathless and flushed.

"Napkins?" Teresa broke away from the embrace with a rakish grin.

"In the top cabinet to the left of the sink."

Maddy couldn't help looking at Teresa's backside. She was stretched up, her T-shirt revealing the smooth flesh of her belly, and Maddy suppressed the urge to slide her hands underneath the fabric to cup Teresa's breasts.

"Here." Teresa tossed down the napkins.

"Do you want wine?"

"No, thanks. I'll have some water."

Maddy poured herself a glass of red, and they divided the pizza.

Teresa was relaxed, and she decided that it was a good time to satisfy more of her curiosity about Maddy.

"Why did your girlfriend cheat on you?"

"What?"

"Why did Christine cheat on you?"

Teresa saw Maddy's posture stiffen as she leaned back in her chair and stopped eating.

"I guess she got bored and was looking for more excitement than I could give her."

"Bored? You're certainly anything but boring." Teresa pulled another slice of pizza from the box and set it on her plate. *You're*

passionate and generous, sincere and intelligent, anything but boring.
"You two had a relationship, and she was unfaithful."

"That's about it in a nutshell." Maddy took a bite of her pizza and sat back as she chewed it with a thoughtful expression on her face. "I was starting my first job as a grammar school teacher, and Christine was an up-and-coming litigation attorney with big clients to schmooze."

"So."

"She never understood that when you're a teacher the day doesn't end just because school is over. You don't just teach the kids in your class. You end up working with the families, too. There was always a student in crisis at home, and whatever happened at home affected the kid in school. Sometimes that meant meeting parents after work."

"I can attest to that. She knew this was what you were going to do once you graduated. Right?"

"Yeah..."

"How long did you know each other before you moved in together?"

"We met my senior year. So it wasn't quite a year." Maddy picked up her pizza and took a bite.

"You both knew what the working situation was going to be like."

"Sure, I did."

"So, let me get this straight. Christine's the hotshot litigation attorney who works atrociously long days, and she's the one who has a problem with the hours that you put in as a teacher?"

"She wanted me to be home when she was. Her vacations didn't always coincide with mine."

"It all sounds a little controlling to me."

"At first, it didn't seem that way. She wanted us to spend time together."

"And when that didn't happen, she used that as an excuse to step over the line."

"Christine had been with Tina for months before I even knew they were having an affair."

Teresa's voice was gentle. "And she dumped the blame for her infidelity at your feet."

Maddy looked across the table at Teresa. "How do you know she blamed me?"

"I can see how upset it still makes you. And, and you forget that I met her once already."

Maddy took a gulp of her wine and nodded miserably. "Well, you're right. She did blame me, and then she lied to me about the affair."

"She broke your heart." Teresa took Maddy's hand and squeezed it. "How did you find out she was cheating?"

"She'd been putting in a lot of late hours and had been coming home exhausted. I thought I would do something nice and take her dinner to her after work one day. I showed up after work and her assistant looked at me as if I had six heads. She proceeded to tell me that Christine had left two hours ago with Tina Pedicini. I knew right then and there something was wrong."

"Why?"

"There were phone calls that she would take into another room at home. She talked about Tina too much. There were charges on the credit card that I questioned her about. Christine said she lost her business credit card and had to put some client dinners on ours."

"You didn't believe her."

"Not when there were dinners charged at a well-known gay bar in the Village."

"Was she stupid?"

"No, I think it got to the point where she just didn't care anymore."

"What did you do?"

"I waited for her to come home one night. I was going to confront her, but before I got up the courage to do it, she told me she was moving out. She said she was in love with Tina and had been seeing her for months. I said some terrible things. The rest of the year sucked. I spent weekends coming to New Jersey to visit Angela. That's when she convinced me to look for a job closer to her."

"So you moved out here."

"I was running away, or so I thought. My aunt died in the middle of Christine and me breaking up. She left this property to me. The same week I drove out here and looked at the barn and the land for the first time, I got an interview at Brian's grammar school."

Teresa balled up her napkin and dropped it onto her plate. "Let me ask you something. Are you seeing anybody else?"

"No."

Teresa was quiet as she absorbed this information.

Maddy shook her head. "No, I'm not. Is that what you want?"

It dawned on Teresa, as she sat there listening to Maddy, she didn't want to share this woman who had touched her heart with anyone else. "Before I met you," she said, "I hadn't even thought about being with anyone again."

"And now?"

"I enjoy the time we've spent together. When we're apart, all I can think about is seeing you again."

Maddy let out a long breath, as she looked into the hazel eyes and listened to the slightly husky timbre of Teresa's voice. She felt herself drawn to Teresa and was helpless to fight the feelings stirring deep inside. "I don't mind us seeing just each other. I'd like to think we have a chance at something together."

Teresa looked at Maddy and smiled into her eyes. "I guess we'll find out."

"We'll take it day by day. So, you'll let me know about Saturday."

Teresa stood up and took her plate to the sink. "I'll know by tomorrow afternoon."

"I have a suggestion." Maddy moved closer to Teresa and laid a palm against Teresa's cheek. "If Brian can stay with Betty and Rich, why don't you come over here and spend the night?"

"I'd like that."

"It looks like that rain is letting up."

Teresa glanced out the window. "So it is."

Maddy slipped her other arm around Teresa's waist and kissed her soundly on the lips. "Go, before I drag you into my bed."

Maddy watched Teresa as she walked through the door. She was surprised at the sensation of helpless yearning that filled her heart when Teresa's truck finally disappeared from view. So, what *was* "having a chance at something"? Was she talking about falling in love with Teresa? Maddy wasn't sure she was ready to let her life head in that direction again, and she wondered for a moment if Teresa was.

Chapter
Thirteen

SINCE TERESA WAS back in town on Friday, she stopped at the hardware store to pick up supplies. The electrical and plumbing inspections were scheduled for later in the afternoon. If both went well, she could bring a crew in to install the insulation and sheet rock on Saturday. The whole interior of the house would be complete in a day and a half. After that, it would take a few days for the taping and spackling to be finished, and then she could start the finishing work.

She picked out a few pieces of trim and door handles for Maddy to choose from and headed to the counter at the front of the store.

"Morning, Ed," she said, as the storeowner finished with another customer.

"Hi, Teresa. How's Rich doing? I heard the call on the police radio last week."

"He's home and recuperating."

"That's good to hear. That must have given you quite a scare."

"Yes, it did."

"Did you get everything you needed?"

"Yeah, can you check on a delivery of drywall for Saturday?" She handed him a credit card.

"Sure. Let me run this through." As he waited for the machine to process his request, Ed flipped through a clipboard hanging above the counter. "I've got you down as our first delivery on Saturday morning."

"Excellent. Thanks, Ed."

"Give Rich my regards, and tell him not to slack off too long."

"I will," Teresa said with a laugh and a wave.

After she placed her purchases in the truck, she checked her watch. It was 11:15, and since she had skipped breakfast, she decided to eat at the diner across the street. It was rare for her to have an opportunity to spend any time alone, so she asked for a corner booth away from the door.

She gave a cursory glance at the menu and set it down on the table. It was too early for the lunch crowd, so many of the tables were empty.

She looked up as the waitress walked to her table and thumbed through several pages of her order pad.

"What can I get you, hon?"

"I'll have bacon, lettuce, and tomato on wheat toast and a large glass of milk."

"Is that all?"

"That's it." Teresa handed back the menu.

While she waited, she pulled out her cell phone and keyed in Maddy's number. "Hi, Maddy. It's Teresa. Brian's going to stay over at Rich and Betty's, so I'll see you Saturday. Let me know what time you want me to come over."

Teresa settled back in her seat and watched several people walk through the entrance. To her absolute astonishment, Erin walked in a moment later behind two businessmen.

A tall, fit, attractive woman, Erin was dressed in an expensive gray business suit with high heels to match. Slung over her shoulder was a stylish leather briefcase. A headband pulled her hair back, and her wispy bangs perfectly framed her freckled face.

If Teresa could have willed herself to be invisible, she would have. All her wishing was to no avail, though, because Erin turned and glanced directly at her.

A look of shock crossed Erin's face, followed by a flicker of emotion that was too fleeting for Teresa to make out whether it was uneasiness or curiosity.

Teresa tried to keep her expression neutral as Erin approached from across the diner. She was grateful for the small favor that at least Brian wasn't with her.

"Hello, Teresa."

"Hi, Erin." Teresa tried to hide her irritation as she watched Erin slide into the seat across from her.

"This is a surprise, meeting you here." Piercing blue eyes, made more dramatic by flawlessly applied makeup, studied Teresa's face.

"Well, I guess it was bound to happen sooner or later. It's not like you moved out of the state."

"It's been a long time."

Not long enough. Teresa remained silent. She couldn't help the little scenes that played in her mind of the happier times they had spent together. She mentally shook her head to clear the memories.

Erin offered a conciliatory smile. "How's Brian doing?"

"As well as can be expected." Teresa folded her arms on the

table in front of her.

"What about you? How are you doing?"

"I'm doing okay."

"That's it?" Erin asked.

"What do you expect me to say? It's been a year and a half since you left. Life goes on."

"You've been on my mind lately. You don't just stop caring about someone you spent five years of your life with, Teresa."

"You had a strange way of showing it."

Erin pressed her lips together in a thin line. "It was a terrible time for all of us."

"I'm glad I know how you felt about it." Teresa glared at her.

Teresa's tone and expression should have warned Erin that she had crossed a line and it was time to back off. "We had something good together. I haven't forgotten that, and I'm sure you haven't, either."

"You were the one who chose to leave." Teresa tried to sound unaffected by Erin's words.

"Teresa, I tried to be honest and up front about what I wanted. You never would listen. I think we all have limits as to what we're able to tolerate."

Teresa huffed out an angry breath. "You have no right to walk in here and talk to me about limits."

"I had a right to live my life. I didn't have to agree with all of your choices. You didn't involve me, Teresa. You made the decisions by yourself."

Both women looked up as the waitress returned with Teresa's sandwich.

"If you don't mind, I'll take that to go."

"Oh, okay. Anything for you, ma'am?" The waitress glanced between the two women.

"No, I won't be staying," Erin said, and the waitress left.

For a long time, Teresa didn't answer Erin's charge. Then she said, "No, I didn't involve you. The truth is, I didn't want your help making the decisions I had to make after the accident. It was too painful and confusing. I'm sorry for that."

"I...I'm sorry, too. Maybe I can come see you and Brian sometime."

Teresa's expression hardened. "I think that would be very confusing for him."

"Oh." Erin paused. "Are you involved with someone?"

Teresa hesitated, unsure whether to share this information with Erin, and then decided she didn't care. "Yes, I am."

"Well, maybe you and I can be friends again one day."

Shaking inside, Teresa leaned forward across the table as her temper exploded. "God, you just don't get it do you? You broke Brian's heart when you left. If you think I'm going to give you the opportunity to waltz back into his life and then disappear again when things aren't to your liking, you're wrong."

"There's no need for you to be so mean." Erin gaped at Teresa. She sat back and brushed away a tear that trickled down her cheek. "I've changed, Teresa. I'm not the same person I was then."

"Neither am I. I have to leave now." Teresa stood up abruptly, threw a couple of dollars on the table, and left Erin sitting in the booth wearing a wounded expression on her face. Teresa hastily paid for her sandwich at the register and bolted out of the diner without waiting for her change.

She wasn't one to burn bridges with people, but Erin had betrayed more than just her trust. She had hurt Brian when he was most vulnerable, and *that* she could never forgive or forget. Teresa waited for the light to turn and then hurried across the street to her truck.

She opened the door. Her appetite gone, she tossed the bag with her sandwich across the seat, and climbed inside. Her rage gave way to a sickening realization that Erin had no insight about what impact her leaving had on Brian. Teresa rested her head on the steering wheel and let out a choked sob. Angrily, she rubbed her palms over her eyes to wipe away the tears that had welled up without warning.

Her hand trembled as she fumbled the key into the ignition. She felt the pent up anger and old hurts of betrayal rage inside her. The eight-cylinder engine roared to life, and the tires squealed on the pavement as Teresa pulled out, intent on putting as much distance between her and Erin as possible.

ALREADY IN A sour mood, Teresa spent the better part of the afternoon at Maddy's house with the plumbing and electrical inspector. The plumbing inspector arrived late and was determined to nitpick every conceivable point he could with Sam.

Teresa took care of a couple of calls while she waited for the two of them to finish their verbal sparring over different aspects of the plumbing code. She decided that she was going to have a heart-to-heart talk with Rich about using Sam's services in the future. They certainly didn't need Sam's problems carrying over into their business.

After the inspector left, Sam wasted no time. He walked up to Teresa and stood in front of her with arms folded over his chest.

"Where's my money?"

"You'll get it after you hear what I have to say."

Sam rolled his eyes heavenward and heaved a sigh.

"I don't get you, Sam. What do you think you're going to gain by pissing off the customers and the inspectors?"

"The inspector at the Wilson's project didn't know his ass from his elbow."

"So, have some tact instead of shoving that fact in his face. Word gets around quickly in this business. Rich is your bread and butter. Without him, your workload goes down by half and you know it."

"Don't threaten me, Teresa."

"I'm not. Just understand you're not the only game in town, and I will not have you screwing with our reputation. We have a good relationship with the inspectors because they know we do good work. I intend to keep it that way."

"When did Rich leave you in charge?"

"While he's at home recuperating, you go through me." She pulled out an envelope and handed it to him.

Sam glowered at her but took the envelope and left without another word.

It was as if a weight lifted from her shoulders as Teresa acknowledged with a sigh of relief that the week was finally over, and all she had to look forward to was spending tonight with Brian.

BRIAN FIDGETED AS he sat on the couch beside Teresa. He enjoyed being with her on Friday nights. She would usually order pizza and rent a movie they could watch together until it was time for bed.

He wriggled as Teresa leaned over and planted a kiss on the top of his head.

"Are you tired, Brian?"

He kept blinking and the movie was getting fuzzy. "Yeah, I think I just want to go to bed." He climbed off the couch and yawned.

"Go on. I'll be in, in a few minutes. Don't forget to brush your teeth."

"Okay."

Brian trudged into the bathroom and stared at his toothbrush. He really didn't feel like brushing his teeth tonight. He ran the brush under the water, shook it so he splattered water around the sink, and set the brush back in its holder.

He scrambled into his bed and sat for a moment, thinking. He flopped onto his stomach and hung over the edge of the mattress. He stretched his arm out and retrieved a photo album that he kept underneath his bed.

Some nights when he awoke, he would turn his bedside lamp on and dig the scrapbook out. He set it on his lap and opened the cover.

The first picture was of his mom and dad holding him when he was a little baby. Pictures of him, his parents, and his Aunt Teresa filled the pages. With an intent gaze, he pulled the photos closer and then held them at arm's length. The pictures progressed until the summer he turned four years old.

One picture showed his birthday party, and he was sitting on his mom's lap blowing out the candles on his cake. She had gotten him his favorite, chocolate cake with chocolate pudding inside and whipped cream icing. Brian smoothed his fingers over his mother's face. His belly ached when he looked at the picture, and his eyes started to burn.

He could remember sitting in the front pew next to Teresa listening to the minister talk. Brian couldn't recall anything the man said that day or understand many of the words, but he knew he was talking about his mom and dad. It was crowded and hot in the church, and a lot of people were crying.

Aunt Teresa was crying, too. He didn't want her to cry because *that* scared him. Everyone had told him that his mom and dad had an accident, and they were with the angels in heaven. He didn't know what heaven was or where he could find it. All he knew was that he wanted his mom and dad to come back home.

He let out a sob and buried his face in his pillow. He didn't want Teresa to hear him crying. She cried, too, sometimes, but she did it when she thought she was alone. He had seen her crying, and that awful feeling of being scared and terribly alone would come back to him.

"Brian?"

He wiped his face on his pillow and sniffled loudly. He felt his mattress shift and saw Teresa sitting on the edge of his bed.

He watched as she lifted the photo album and studied the picture he had been looking at.

"Do you know what I remember about your birthday?"

He shook his head. "What?"

"I remember how excited you were to get your new bicycle."

"I learned how to ride it without training wheels by the end of the summer."

"Yes, you did. You couldn't wait to show me."

"You showed me how to pop a wheelie."

"Yeah, your mom wasn't too happy with me for showing you that."

"Dad said it was all right as long as I didn't do them in the street." Brian sat up and turned the pages back to the photo that showed him sitting with his parents on the beach. "I like this picture."

"That was a fun trip," Teresa said, surprised at the swell of emotion that brought tears to her eyes.

"How come Aunt Erin was afraid to go swimming in the ocean?"

"I think she was afraid of what might be in the water."

"You mean like sharks and manta rays and big giant squids?"

"Aunt Erin didn't like to swim unless she could see the bottom of a pool."

"That's silly."

"Not really. Some people are afraid of the ocean."

Brian was quiet as he looked up at Teresa's face, and then in a solemn voice he asked, "Why did Aunt Erin leave us?"

Out of the mouths of babes, Teresa thought, as her throat constricted with emotion. "I think there were a lot of reasons."

"Like what?"

"Do you know how sometimes you get upset with your friends because they do something that you don't like or something that hurts you?"

"Yeah, like when Steven took my ball and wouldn't give it back."

"Well, sort of like that. When you're an adult, the problems are bigger and harder to solve. People can't always work their problems out."

"Is that what happened to you and Aunt Erin?"

"Yes, I guess it did. My grandmother used to say, 'Little people, little problems. Big people, big problems.'"

"Do big people always have problems?"

"No, not always."

"Good, 'cause I don't think I want to get big if they do."

Brian curled up on his side and laid his head on the pillow.

"Do you want to keep this album under your pillow tonight?"

Brian shook his head and pulled the album into his arms. "I'll keep it right here."

"That's fine." Teresa brushed her fingers through his hair. "It's okay to feel sad about your mom and dad." Teresa's voice was soft and sweet. "It's okay to cry if you want. Sometimes it's the only thing that makes me feel better."

"When you cry, do you feel better?"

"Sometimes. A good cry lets the hurt that I feel on the inside come out."

"Will it always hurt so much, Teresa?"

"I think the sadness changes, and maybe it feels different over time."

Brian yawned and pulled the album tight in his arms. "Tomorrow, when I go to Aunt Betty's..."

He was asleep before he could finish his sentence. Teresa kissed the side of his head and gently tucked the covers around him. She gazed back at him and turned the light off before she closed his bedroom door.

Chapter
Fourteen

THE WEATHER WAS starting to turn to late fall, Teresa decided as she walked along the sidewalk of downtown Morristown on Saturday afternoon. She had noticed it in the clouds and the color of the sky earlier in the week. Little odd-shaped clouds that seemed to stand still in the deep blue sky for hours replaced the billowy fair-weather clouds of late summer and early fall. Cool, crisp air, and brilliant sun shining through a deep blue sky took the place of the hazy humidity that New Jersey was famous for.

This was one of her favorite times of year. Sweatshirt weather. That's what David used to call it. It was the short lull of activity that fell between the first few weeks of school when everyone's schedules were crazy, and the eventual build-up to the holidays when there never seemed to be enough time to get everything done.

She scanned the stores that lined the sidewalks. She didn't like going empty-handed when she was invited to someone's home. At the liquor store, she had purchased a bottle of cabernet sauvignon, and now she was searching for something else that she could take to Maddy. She stopped outside one of the florist shops and decided that flowers were her best option.

She opened the door and listened to the bell chime as she stepped inside.

A young girl appeared a moment later from the back room. "Can I help you with something?"

"I'd like to get a bouquet of flowers, something with reds, blues, and yellows in it. I don't want red roses, though."

"That's no problem. We have some red Gerbera daisies that will go nicely with the other colors you want."

"Great."

Teresa picked out the flowers that she wanted, and then surveyed the myriad of garden supplies while she waited for the girl to wrap up her selection.

"Is that it?"

"Yes, thank you." Teresa held out her credit card.

SHE ARRIVED AT Maddy's shortly after six. She was surprised when Maddy met her at the corner of the barn with a basket of freshly picked vegetables. She could smell the pungent scent of the ripe tomatoes.

"Wow, those are all from your garden?"

"Yes, they are. Ooh, those flowers are beautiful." She leaned in, inhaled their perfume, and then touched her mouth to the corner of Teresa's.

"Come on up, and I'll give you a proper greeting." Maddy looked at Teresa with a mischievous sparkle in her eyes.

Teresa followed her up the stairs and into the apartment. She set the flowers on the counter while Maddy carefully deposited her bounty into the sink.

"I missed you," Maddy said, as she gave her hands a quick scrub under the faucet. After she dried her hands and tossed the towel down, she slipped her arms around Teresa's waist and kissed her deeply.

Teresa stroked her fingers through Maddy's hair. She traced the tips of her fingers down the curve of Maddy's neck, over her shoulders, and rested them lightly on her hips. She felt the burn start down deep inside her.

Maddy pulled away and smiled at Teresa through slightly glazed eyes. "If we keep that up, we're not going to eat dinner."

"We could skip straight to dessert."

Maddy couldn't remember a time when she felt a connection like this with someone, and she knew that Teresa could feel it, too. "No, I need food first. I made chicken *cordon blue* and a salad."

"That sounds delicious."

"I hope so. I haven't made it in a while." Maddy stepped away from their embrace and let her fingers twine with Teresa's for a brief moment. "Would you mind getting the plates out while I fix the flowers in a vase?"

Teresa decided she felt content to be doing this, as she retrieved the plates from the cabinet. Just the simple act of sharing dinner with Maddy made her feel good inside. A part of her wished Brian was with her to share in this moment. She didn't think Maddy would have objected, but that was for another time.

As she set the table, Teresa watched Maddy. She liked the way that Maddy's smile lit up her face and the sure, quick movements of her hands as she trimmed the flowers and set them in the vase. She liked Maddy's sharp wit and her soft tenderness, and she found her warm sensuality captivating.

"A penny for your thoughts." Maddy glanced over her shoulder at Teresa.

Teresa bit back an outburst of laughter, and she felt a flush quickly heat her cheeks. "Nothing in particular." She quickly changed the subject. "Have you thought about hiring someone to paint your new place, or are you going to do it yourself?"

"I don't know yet," she said, finding herself enamored by Teresa's reaction. "I would probably try to do it myself. I think hiring someone would be really expensive."

"You're right about that. The good thing is you have this apartment, so you don't have to be in a rush if you want to take the time and paint it yourself."

"I think I'd like to use some of the same colors I have in here, maybe some softer tones in the upstairs. I'm open to suggestions, if you have any."

"I'll give it some thought." Teresa looked around the room and mentally catalogued the colors Maddy liked.

Maddy opened the oven door and checked on the chicken. "I think we're all done here. Can you get the salad? It's on the second shelf of the refrigerator."

THE CHICKEN WAS cooked to perfection, and the salad Maddy served was drizzled with garlic and Parmesan dressing she made from scratch earlier that day.

"Dinner was great, Maddy. Thank you."

"You're welcome."

Teresa speared her last piece of chicken *cordon blue* and savored it as she chewed it slowly.

"It's nice to be able to cook for somebody other than myself." Maddy took a sip of her wine and set the glass down. "Why don't we clean up the table, and then we can relax on the couch?"

They spent about twenty minutes cleaning up the kitchen and putting the leftovers away.

"Do you think Brian would like this?" Maddy asked, as she pulled out a container to put the remaining chicken in.

"It's got everything he likes in it. I'm sure he would."

"Well here, I'll put these two in here for you and him. Have them Monday night."

Taken aback by her offer, Teresa hesitated. "Maddy, you don't have to do that."

"I know, but I want to."

"It won't go to waste, that's for sure."

Maddy rinsed her hands under the water and then dried them off with a paper towel. "Do you want some more wine?"

"I'd love some," Teresa replied.

Maddy filled their glasses and handed one to Teresa. "It was chilly out, so I brought some wood in for a fire."

"What a great idea. Do you want some help?"

"No, I've got it." Maddy set her wineglass on the end table. She knelt in front of the wood-burning stove, opened the glass door, and arranged some crumpled newspaper and kindling inside. She lit a match and little flames burnt the edges of the paper and leapt up to the twigs. She pulled a couple of small logs out of the box she kept in the corner, set them inside, and shut the door.

When she joined Teresa on the couch, she leaned against Teresa's slightly taller frame and rested her head on her shoulder.

Teresa dipped her chin slightly and glanced down, smiling at the sensation of Maddy's cheek resting just above her breast and Maddy's body relaxing against hers.

Maddy slid her hand under Teresa's and lifted it up. Despite the hard work that Teresa did, she had beautiful hands, with short, well-manicured nails. Strong hands that had explored her body intimately and left her aching to feel them on her again. Hearing Teresa's voice so close in her ear had an electrifying effect on her senses, and her gaze met Teresa's.

Teresa said, "You haven't shared with me yet the significance of your nickname."

Maddy rolled her eyes in mock horror. "I was hoping you might have forgotten about it."

"Forget your sister calling you 'Mad Dog Geddes'? I don't think so."

Maddy lowered Teresa's hand and sat up. "It's from my rugby-playing days."

Teresa looked at Maddy with a comical expression on her face. "*You* played rugby?"

"Yes, I played in college for a couple of years and then on a club team after I graduated."

"What position did you play?"

"I was a flanker because I was fast and could lay a mean tackle on the other team's ball carrier."

Teresa laughed. "I wouldn't have expected that to be a sport that you played."

"Well, it's going back quite a few years."

Teresa lifted her wineglass to her lips and said, "So, how did you acquire your nickname?"

"Obviously, I'm not that big, but what I didn't have in size I made up for by being fast and aggressive. I used to growl at the other players when I was going after the ball."

Teresa coughed on her wine. "Growl? As in baring your teeth

and growling like a dog?"

"More like a rabid dog with a feral gleam in its eyes is how one of my teammates described it to me."

Teresa chuckled. "Did it work?"

"If you can imagine a mud-covered, adrenaline-crazed lesbian flinging her body at the legs of the opposing team's ball carrier and knocking the ball loose, then yeah, I would say it worked quite nicely."

"That's a frightening description." Teresa struggled to reconcile the image of the Maddy she knew with a Maddy covered in mud and tackling another woman on a torn-up rugby field.

"My mother and sister were horrified when they first saw me play. Of course, after a few games, Angela was leading the team chanting 'Mad Dog, Mad Dog' when I would make an open-field tackle."

"I wish I could have seen you play."

"Ask Angela one day. She probably still has a couple of games on tape hanging around somewhere."

Teresa leaned in and kissed Maddy soundly on the lips. "It certainly rounds out my image of you."

"Hopefully, it's not tarnished."

"No, I like a woman who can handle herself."

Maddy reached for her glass and took a sip of her wine. "So do I."

She set her glass down and came back for Teresa's lips. The taste of wine and spice mingled with the scent of Teresa's perfume and stirred a desire deep inside Maddy. She pulled Teresa tightly against her.

Teresa was so lost in the kiss she couldn't help the dismayed expression on her face when Maddy pulled away.

"I think we'll enjoy the next part of the evening better if we go into the bedroom."

Chapter
Fifteen

TERESA AWOKE TO the sun sending slivers of light over her face and dancing over her eyes. Disoriented at first, she lifted her head to look around the neatly kept bedroom that wasn't her own. She was alone, the covers thrown back where Maddy had slept beside her through the night.

She heard rustling sounds coming from the direction of the kitchen and wondered how long Maddy had been awake. The smell of fresh coffee floated in, and her stomach rumbled as she sat up in bed.

She threw back the covers and walked to the bathroom. She was washing her hands and splashing water on her face when she felt a presence behind her. She looked up from drying her face with a towel and caught Maddy's smiling reflection in the mirror.

"Good morning." Maddy pushed off the wall and walked over to Teresa, appreciating the view of her naked body as she approached. "Did you sleep well?"

"I don't think I moved."

Maddy slipped a hand into Teresa's and led her back to the bedroom. She wrapped her arms around Teresa and nestled her head against Teresa's chest. "Neither did I. That was, um...incredible last night."

Teresa laughed, trying to ignore the effect Maddy's touch was having on her. Her body was already unmistakably aroused, and Maddy stroking her hand across her bare buttocks definitely did not help. "I...God, I don't think I can form a coherent thought with you doing that."

"You mean this?" Maddy trailed one of her hands over Teresa's hips and dipped lower, touching the thick curls of hair that were moistened with the juices of Teresa's arousal.

"You're even more beautiful when you're aroused."

A flush of heat colored Teresa's cheeks, and she was suddenly self-conscious of her nakedness.

"Ohhh! Maddy...please...I'll die from wanting you."

"We can't have that now, can we?"

Maddy's lips and hands moved over Teresa's body, tormenting and tantalizing. Teresa clutched Maddy's shoulders, and her back arched as Maddy entered her fully. Her legs buckled, and she sank to her knees, taking Maddy with her.

Teresa's hips were undulating wildly, and she begged, "Please, please," repeatedly.

Maddy felt her fingers squeezed by Teresa's muscles, and she was pulled deeper into her. Their lovemaking was ardent and swift. In the span of several heartbeats, Teresa was lost to the passion.

She moaned in delight and clutched Maddy tightly as she rode the crest of her orgasm. Her cry was captured by Maddy's mouth hard against hers, and a heart-searing sense of blessedness filled her.

Long moments passed before Teresa opened her eyes, and her breathing returned to normal. Maddy gently held her face in both hands and rubbed a thumb over her full and tender lips before kissing them softly.

Something caught in the back of Maddy's throat as she drew back and gazed into Teresa's sultry eyes. Her heart told her even if she could not form the words. And that was the problem, wasn't it? What she had said she wasn't ready for, what she had sworn she didn't want to happen had crept into her heart and soul and left her defenseless. She loved Teresa.

Teresa seemed to sense her discomfort and, thinking that Maddy was cold, dragged the blanket from the bed.

"Here." She settled the cover over Maddy's shoulders and helped her to her feet. They stood in the center of the bedroom, and Teresa wrapped her arms around Maddy in a fierce hug.

"Thank you." Maddy held back a sob as a wave of emotion ripped through her.

Teresa rubbed her hands in lazy circles over Maddy's back. Teresa knew what she wanted to say, but she held back. She was the one with the six-year-old child, and somehow that made her afraid to hope Maddy might be feeling the same emotions she was.

"Hey, I smelled coffee when I woke up," Teresa said, deliberately trying to lighten the tension in the room. She stepped away from Maddy and slipped her discarded nightshirt over her head.

"I put a pot on when I heard you get up. You must be famished. I know I am."

A smile edged up the corner of Teresa's mouth. "It must have been all the activity."

Maddy laughed and tugged her out of the bedroom.

"Come on, I'll make scrambled eggs. I took a mango out of the refrigerator that you can cut up."

Maddy cracked four eggs into a bowl and whisked them with a fork.

Teresa pulled a knife out of a drawer and cut a wedge of the mango and peeled back the skin. "Mmm, taste this." She slid a piece of the sweet-tasting fruit over Maddy's lips before slipping it slowly into her mouth.

"You're such a tease," Maddy said. "That's delicious."

Teresa poured them each a mug of coffee and doled a spoonful of sugar into hers along with some milk. "How do you take yours?"

"Just sugar." Maddy glanced at Teresa and wondered what she thought about their burgeoning relationship, and what, if anything, she had told Brian.

Sensing the subtle change in Maddy's mood, Teresa studied her. She had experienced the most exciting and satisfying sexual experiences of her life with this woman. There was definitely chemistry between them, there was no doubt, but she wondered how that mutual attraction and understanding would withstand a long-term relationship, and the demands of raising a six-year-old.

"Teresa, have you said anything to Brian about us?"

Teresa handed Maddy her mug. "Just that we were having dinner. He asked a couple of questions on his own last week."

"Like what?"

Teresa lifted her coffee cup to her lips to hide the amused smile that was starting. "He wanted to know what first base was."

"He what?" Maddy stared at Teresa, her mouth agape. "He's only in first grade."

Teresa's eyes shined with laughter. "That was about my reaction, then I remembered that the friend he stayed with last weekend has an older brother."

"Oh, I don't know if that makes me feel any better or not. How much do you think he understood about you and Erin?" Maddy asked, suddenly feeling a little wary.

"I don't know. We told him that we loved each other, and he knew we lived in the same house. Of course, up until David and Fran died, we were Aunt T and Aunt Erin to him."

Maddy was silent for a moment as she poured the eggs into the hot pan. "That must have been awful for him when Erin left."

"It was." Teresa pulled two plates out of one of the cabinets and set them on the counter. "I actually bumped into Erin on Thursday at the diner in town."

"You did?" Maddy looked at Teresa.

"She asked if she could come by and see Brian someday."

"What did you tell her?" Maddy tilted the pan to cover it with the eggs.

"That I thought it would be confusing for him. I told her she was crazy if she thought I was going to give her the chance to waltz into his life again."

"Are you always that blunt?"

"When it comes to that particular issue, I am."

"What did she say?"

"She cried and thought I was being mean to her." Teresa ran her thumb over the rim of the coffee mug that was in her hands. "Maybe I am, and it's my way of getting back at her for pouring salt into an open wound, but she doesn't have any idea what it was like to experience the absolute, utter grief that consumed Brian for months. I know I'm partly to blame for her leaving. I was in a terrible place for a long time, and I'm sure I wasn't pleasant to live with."

"Maybe not, but you were grieving, too, while trying to be a parent at the same time."

"What's done is done. I wouldn't change any of the decisions I made."

"Hand me a plate. The eggs are ready."

"Do you want another cup of coffee?" Teresa held out a plate to Maddy.

"I'd love one."

They ate breakfast and drank their coffee while they talked about their plans for the day. The sunlight was bright, but the brisk wind that was rustling the branches of the trees was the kind that carried a nip.

Teresa felt content and relaxed sitting next to Maddy. She thought they were creating something together that was more than just a fling; maybe they were making a place for each other in their hearts.

Maddy leaned back in her chair and looked at Teresa. A month ago, she thought Teresa looked worn and tired, as if she were struggling to make it through each day. There was still sadness in those eyes, but Maddy had seen the veil of weariness lift last night.

On some level, she wanted to see more of that, so she leaned forward and asked, "What are you going to do with Brian today?"

"Say that again?" Teresa pulled herself back from daydreaming.

"What are your plans with Brian today?"

"It depends on if Betty wants us to stay for dinner."

"Oh."

Teresa didn't miss the hint of disappointment in Maddy's voice, and she took a moment to consider this before she responded. "After we finish here, I'll call Betty and find out what they're planning to do today. Maybe we can all spend the day together."

Maddy immediately said, "I'd like that."

PART OF TERESA would have been perfectly content to continue lounging in Maddy's apartment and making love throughout the day, but that wasn't going to happen now. She called Betty, who was in the middle of making an apple pie.

"Hi, Betty."

"I didn't expect to hear from you until later. Is everything all right?"

"Everything's fine. What's Brian up to?"

"He's out back keeping Rich company."

"Betty, do you mind if Maddy joins us for dinner?"

"Absolutely not. Of course, Maddy can join us. I'm making a pot roast, so there will be plenty of food to go around."

"Do you want us to bring anything?"

"Just your appetites."

SITTING IN MADDY'S leather chair, casually looking at the pictures in one of her magazines, Teresa waited for her to finish dressing so they could leave for Betty and Rich's house.

After breakfast, they had gone back to bed, made love again, and afterward fell into a deep slumber. Teresa woke shortly before noon with Maddy in her arms. She felt very content lying there, and she still felt that way now.

"Sorry I took so long," Maddy said, as she walked out of the bedroom.

Teresa looked up, her smile turning into an appreciative grin. Maddy looked incredibly sexy, dressed in a flattering pair of blue jeans, a white short-sleeved T-shirt, and sneakers.

"I didn't give Betty a specific time, so we're fine."

"That was a good idea, considering..." Maddy stopped directly in front of Teresa and looked at her with a warm smile.

Teresa stood up, smiling back at Maddy, and she slipped her hands around Maddy's waist in a light caress. "I thought so, too. Hi."

"Hi," Maddy whispered and gently pressed her lips against Teresa's in a friendly kiss. "Let's get out of here."

They left shortly after two o'clock and made the drive across town in fifteen minutes. The enticing aroma of baked apples and cinnamon drifted out of the open kitchen window as they got out of Teresa's truck.

"That smells absolutely heavenly," Maddy said.

"Hello?" Teresa stepped up onto the front porch and peered inside the screen door.

"Come on in. I'm in the kitchen," Betty called.

"It smells wonderful in here," Maddy said.

Betty was wearing a red apron over her yellow T-shirt and jeans. She held her hands out and embraced Maddy with a hug. "I'm so glad you could come for dinner, Maddy."

"Thanks for having me over."

Betty turned to Teresa and hugged her, too. "Brian watched movies and ate popcorn with Uncle Rich last night."

"I'm sure he loved that."

"He did. He insisted that he stayed awake all night, but he was conked out on the couch by 10:30 when I checked on him."

"Where are they now?" Teresa asked.

"I think Rich is teaching Brian to tie lures and set bait on a fishing hook."

"They're going fishing?" Maddy asked.

"If that's what you want to call it. It's more like an excuse to hang out in the boat for a couple of hours while the pot roast cooks."

The screen door opened and banged noisily behind Rich. "Good afternoon, ladies."

"Good grief, Rich. Do you think you have enough lures attached to your hat?" Teresa asked.

"Do you like it?" He took it off and handed it to her for closer inspection.

"Like it? There's so much metal on it you could be a lightning rod."

"I hear you and Brian are going fishing," Maddy said.

"Care to join us, Maddy? We won't be far out, mostly in the shallows where the fish sleep in the afternoon."

"I'll come along for a little while."

"Good. I have an extra rod in the shed that you can use."

"It's been years since I fished."

"It's just like riding a bike," Rich said, and then turned when he heard Brian calling to him from outside.

"Uncle Rich, look!" Brian ran up to the screen door and opened it. "I did it." He proudly displayed a night crawler wriggling from the end of his hook.

"Oh, dear Lord, get that out of here, Brian." Betty took several steps away and wrinkled her nose in disgust.

Teresa walked over, kissed Brian on the head, and guided him out the door. "Nice job with the worm."

"Thanks." Brian held up his free hand, and Teresa responded with a high five.

"I think Ms. Geddes is going to come along with you for a while."

"What about you?"

"There's only room for three on the boat, and you need Uncle

Rich to drive it."

"Okay." His face brightened when Maddy walked outside. "Hi, Ms. Geddes."

"Hi, Brian. Do you think you can teach me how to put bait on a hook?"

"It's easy after you practice a few times. Come on." Brian took Maddy's hand and led her over to the dock.

"Have fun," Teresa called and winked at Maddy when she smiled back at her.

"I see a twinkle in your eye that hasn't been there in a while, Teresa," Rich said.

"Could be," she said, with an easy smile.

"I know that look. It's the same one I walked around with after I met Betty." He clapped her on the shoulder and walked toward the dock whistling a slightly off-key tune.

Teresa looked back at the lake as she heard the peal of Brian's laughter. She walked into Betty's kitchen and leaned against the counter, watching as Betty chopped some celery.

"There's beer in the refrigerator if you'd like one."

"I'd love one. Thanks." Teresa retrieved the bottle and twisted the top off. "Let me help with some of the chopping, Betty. You don't have to do all of it."

Betty looked up from her work and smiled. "Brian likes Maddy quite a bit."

Teresa glanced out the back door at the dock. "He seems very comfortable around her."

"That's a good thing."

"It is, considering she's tutoring him."

Betty set her knife down and gave Teresa an appraising look. "It is, considering you've got that look of being head over heels in love."

Teresa coughed as she swallowed her beer. "I do not," she said indignantly.

"Oh, yes, you do."

Teresa pulled out a kitchen chair and slumped into it. "I didn't think it was that obvious," she said. "I'm scared."

"Oh, honey, the only thing you can do is trust your feelings. The way you two look at each other...." Betty waggled her eyebrows and made a kissing noise. "You both got it bad, but that's a good thing."

Teresa buried her face in her hands and groaned in embarrassment. "Betty, stop, please."

Betty relented and sat down across from her. "I remember how it feels. I felt that way after my first kiss with Rich. Still do, as a matter of fact."

Teresa peeked out from behind her hands. "The heart still goes pitter patter and all that?"

Betty gave Teresa a knowing smile. "If you're going to sit in here, you might as well get busy and help me cut up those potatoes in the sink. They're already washed."

Life felt good right at this moment, Teresa mused. She picked up a knife and set about quartering the potatoes.

TERESA AND BETTY spent the rest of the afternoon talking leisurely and recounting old memories. The pot roast had been in the oven for over an hour, and the rich aroma filled the kitchen. Teresa eased the oven open, and she let out a surprised yelp when Betty swatted her across the hips with a dishtowel.

"Keep that oven door closed."

"It smelled so good I couldn't resist."

"Go round up the troops. We're almost ready. Tell Rich to come in. I need him to get the extra serving bowls from the pantry."

When Teresa walked out back, she spotted Rich, Brian, and Maddy clustered around the boat. As she approached, she heard Brian's giggling and the murmur of hushed voices.

When she got close, Maddy and Brian turned around. "Surprise!" They held up a good-sized trout in front of them.

"Wow! That's a beauty. Which one of you caught it?"

"It was a team effort," Rich said.

Teresa gestured toward the splotches of dirt on Brian's shirt. "Did you have to wrestle it to the ground?"

"It put up quite a fight," Rich said. "Brian was hanging over the boat with the net at one point, so we wouldn't lose the fish."

"Well, I am impressed. Rich, Betty wants you to get out the extra serving dishes in the pantry."

"I better get in there. Teresa, there's a bag of ice in the freezer. We can keep the trout on ice while we eat, and I'll clean it later."

"Sure thing. Where do you want me to put it for now?"

"There's a cooler in the shed."

After they got the fish put away and washed up, they finally sat down to dinner. It was a satisfying affair, and Brian stuffed himself with meat, mashed potatoes, and two servings of Betty's apple pie.

Afterward, Teresa and Rich chatted about the different construction projects that were ongoing, Betty and Maddy talked about school, and Brian went out to the living room to watch a football game. When the women went to the kitchen to put the leftovers away, Rich joined Brian in front of the television.

"Teresa, can we go for a walk along the lake?" Brian soon

asked from the doorway.

"Give us a few more minutes to clean up, and then we'll take a walk."

About ten minutes later, Teresa, Maddy, and Brian went outside. They walked down to the small footpath that wound its way along the edge of the lake. To Teresa's complete surprise, Brian took hold of Maddy's hand and led her to some of his favorite spots. They stopped several times and skipped stones across the placid surface of the lake, competing to see who could make their stone go the farthest.

It gradually dawned on Teresa that this was the happiest she had been in a long time. She liked the contented feeling she experienced when the three of them were together, and it made her wonder how Maddy felt about them.

Teresa tilted her head up and gazed at the crystal blue sky. It was a peaceful moment, and she experienced a profound awareness of her brother's spirit all around her. The sensation was comforting, and it blanketed her like a secure, affectionate embrace. Tears slipped unexpectedly from beneath her lashes and slid down her cheeks as the feeling grew stronger, and then slowly ebbed, leaving in its wake a bittersweet ache. She brushed away the tears and looked at Maddy and Brian up ahead.

In the stillness of that instant, she realized something. They were meant to be together. Maybe that was why she felt the way she did about Maddy from the very first time they talked, the sense that they were being drawn together.

Up ahead, Brian lingered at a fork in the path. "Come on, Teresa."

"Are you in a rush to get back to the house?" Teresa asked, as she caught up with them.

"No, I just wanted you here." He linked hands with Maddy and Teresa and walked between them on the trail.

Teresa spared a glance over at Maddy and was surprised to see her smiling back with a shimmer of tears in her eyes. Brian swung their arms back and forth, as he walked along, until he got to the edge of the clearing.

"Last one back's a rotten egg!" he shouted and broke into a sprint.

Maddy put a hand on Teresa's arm to stop her. "Wait. I just wanted to thank you for including me in this today." She leaned in and kissed Teresa on the lips.

Teresa's voice dropped to a hoarse whisper. "You're welcome. I'm glad we could spend this time together."

"Are you ready?"

"For what?"

"To be the rotten egg." Maddy raced back to the house with Teresa only a couple of steps behind her.

They ended up at the back door, doubled over and laughing. A few minutes later, after all the goodbyes, Rich joined Teresa by her truck.

"Here's Brian's fish." He handed her the fillets wrapped in wax paper and plastic inside a plastic bag filled with ice.

"Thank you."

"I have a request to make."

"Name it."

"Can I ride with you next week?" He held his hands up as she started to protest. "All I want to do is go to the different sites and check them out. I can't drive, and sitting at home all day is killing me."

"What does the doctor think?"

"I've been to the grocery store walking up and down the aisles with Betty for Chrissakes. I'm doing the cardiac program, but this would help my head. It's depressing as hell being stuck at home."

"As long as you promise not to do any work or yell at anyone."

"Scout's honor." Rich gave her the three-fingered salute.

Chapter
Sixteen

SINCE BRIAN'S GRAMMAR school was on the way to Rich's house, Teresa decided to drive Brian to school on Monday morning. She made her usual stop at the Dunkin' Donuts for coffee and picked an extra one up in case she ran into Maddy outside the school.

Brian didn't seem to mind the change in their morning routine and chatted excitedly about the fish he had caught the day before.

"Teresa, you should have seen the fishing rod bend. That fish was so strong it almost pulled the pole right out of my hands."

"Did Uncle Rich help you reel it in?"

"No, Ms. Geddes did. That fish was so big it almost didn't fit in the net."

"It sounds like you had a lot of fun."

"Yeah. It was cool."

"I'm glad you thought so." Teresa pulled into the parking lot at the school. She had a strong sense that Maddy was right for her. Brian liked her, too, which was imperative. If he hadn't, Teresa wouldn't have let things go as far as they had already.

Across the parking lot, she could see Maddy's car, a bright flash of yellow against the line of evergreen shrubs that ran along the edge of the playground. A bus pulled in behind her and parked by the side entrance.

"Hey, that's my bus." Brian scrambled to get out of the car to join his friends.

"Hold on a second. Take your backpack."

Teresa carried a cup of coffee with her as she stepped out and took in the throng of school age kids gathering along the sidewalk.

She watched Brian interact with his group of friends and didn't see Maddy walking toward her until she was practically by her side.

"This is a pleasant surprise finding you here."

"Rich wants to ride along with me this week. The school's on the way to his house, so I decided I'll drop Brian off each day. Here,

I brought this coffee for you."

"Ooh, I love Dunkin Donuts coffee. Thank you." Maddy tipped her head toward Teresa. "Can we get together this week?"

"Maybe the three of us can have dinner on Wednesday night."

"I'd like that."

"Great. I'll give you a call, so we can work out the details."

"Okay. I'll see you later."

Teresa called out to Brian and waved. She saw a moment's indecision, and then he broke away from the group of kids. He ran over to Teresa and gave her a hug.

"Bye," Teresa said. "I love you."

"Bye, Aunt Teresa," Brian said, and then kissed her on the cheek. He hugged her tightly and spoke into her ear. "I love you, too."

LATER THAT MORNING, Maddy was outside with her class for recess. She walked among the children as they milled about. One group of girls was playing hopscotch and a trio was jumping rope. Some boys were playing "keep away" with a ball.

She spotted Brian standing off by himself watching the boys as they yelled and chased after each other. Since she had started tutoring him, he had seemed to be more confident with his classmates and more willing to join in the games they played at recess.

Concerned, Maddy walked over to where he was standing. "Brian, what are you doing off by yourself?"

He shrugged and slipped his hands into his pockets. "I don't feel like playing."

"Are you feeling all right?"

"Yeah."

Maddy wasn't sure whether he was telling her the truth, but she decided not to press the issue. She continued to walk around the playground, keeping a watchful eye on the kids, when one of the girls in her class joined her.

Maddy glanced down as the curly-haired girl walked alongside her, obviously working up the courage to ask her a question. "Hi, Caroline."

"Ms. Geddes?"

It amused Maddy when the kids prefaced a real question with her name.

"Yes, Caroline?"

"Why does Brian live with his aunt?"

Caroline was one of the older girls in her first grade class and was not only precocious but keenly perceptive as well.

"Have you asked Brian that question?"

"He wouldn't tell me."

"Well, then you need to respect that he doesn't want to talk about it."

"Oh."

She seemed satisfied with Maddy's explanation, but the brief conversation left Maddy wondering if that was the reason Brian was keeping to himself today. She knew from personal experience how cruel kids could be to each other. The ringing of the bell that signaled the end of recess interrupted her thoughts.

As the day went on, she forgot about what had taken place out on the playground. Her tutoring session with Brian went well, and she was pleased with how he was progressing. She was walking him to the door when she heard her name on the overhead paging system.

"Ms. Geddes, please come to the front office."

"Uh-oh. Are you in trouble, Ms. Geddes?" Brian asked, with a grin.

Maddy laughed as she reached the door and looked outside. "I hope not, Brian. I see your aunt waiting for you. Keep up the hard work. You're doing great."

"Okay."

Maddy walked down the hallway and trotted up the stairs to Betty's office.

"Hi, Betty."

An inexplicable smile touched Betty's lips. "These were just delivered to you a few minutes ago."

"Oh, my. They're beautiful," Maddy said, as she moved closer and admired the vase full of red roses.

"There's a card attached."

"Yes, here it is." Maddy opened the envelope and slid the folded paper out. She felt a tightening in her chest as she read the familiar, strong cursive writing.

What else can I say? I'm sorry.
I've missed you so much, for so long.
Christine

Painful memories popped into her mind. She was beyond the point of needing or wanting answers to questions that had haunted her early on after their breakup. She probably wouldn't believe them anyway, not after everything that Christine had lied about. Maddy quickly tucked the card away in her pants pocket.

"Is everything okay?"

Maddy lifted her gaze from the paper and looked directly at

Betty. "Almost everything. Some people don't know how to take 'no' for an answer." Seeing the stricken expression on Betty's face, Maddy continued quickly, "I had a wonderful time yesterday."

"You're welcome anytime, Maddy," Betty said, her expression softening.

"I know how much Teresa cherishes the time Brian gets to spend with you and Rich, so I appreciated being able to share in that yesterday."

Betty gave Maddy a quick glance, filled with an intuitiveness that unsettled her. "Teresa's been drifting these past two years. You've changed that, Madeline. I see something alive in Teresa now that I haven't seen in a long time. It's taken a lot for her to open herself up and let someone in again."

Maddy leaned in and inhaled the scent of the roses. "I believe you."

Betty touched Maddy's shoulder with the palm of her hand. "Please take care of her."

"I will."

Maddy picked up the flowers and carried them with her to her classroom. She stopped briefly to pick up her bag and then walked outside. She was disappointed to see that Brian and Teresa were already gone. She stopped at the dumpster and tossed the vase with the flowers into it. She dug the card out of her pocket, tore it into small pieces and flung it over the top as well.

TERESA SPENT THE better part of Tuesday taping and spackling drywall seams and nail holes in Maddy's house. At lunchtime, she sent Rich off with one of the guys to check out some other job sites and to get him out from under foot. She was happy that Rich was feeling well enough to get out of the house, but because he wasn't working, he had turned into a regular chatter bug and was slowing her down.

By three o'clock, her shoulders were aching, and she drove into town to take a break and get something to eat. On her way there, she decided to stop at the hardware store and pick up some paint chips for Maddy to look at.

If she timed it right, she would be back right about the time Maddy got home from work. The thought brought a smile to Teresa's lips.

MADDY ARRIVED HOME at four o'clock and felt an immediate pang of disappointment that Teresa wasn't there. She was feeling stressed out from the day and decided to go for a walk down by the pond before going inside.

As she walked, Maddy imagined what the pond would look like with some rhododendrons blooming around its edges next spring. She loved to garden and looked forward to having plants that would color the landscape with their blooms from spring until fall.

The woods around her looked peaceful and serene, but when she concentrated, she could hear the rustlings of birds and small animals.

A car door slamming jolted her from her daydreaming, and Maddy looked over her shoulder. She had been thinking of Teresa a lot during the day and was excited to see her now.

When Christine walked around the corner, Maddy's stomach tied instantly into knots. She froze, her brows furrowed together in disbelief that Christine was here.

"Hello, Maddy. I was hoping I would find you home."

Maddy crossed her arms over her chest. "Why?"

"Did you get the roses I sent you?"

"Yes, I did." Maddy watched Christine, trying to get a sense of what she was up to. "It was an unnecessary gesture."

"I was hoping they might bring back some of the old feelings."

After seven years of living together, of course there are still sentiments, good and bad ones, Maddy thought. There were too many memories, and Maddy couldn't let the conversation go on any longer. She was afraid she would let her defenses down, and Christine might sense an opportunity that wasn't there. "Chris, you can't possibly believe I still love you. I don't know how else to make you understand that there's no chance for us to get back together."

"We could still be friends, see each other, maybe?" Christine's voice softened, as she looked directly at Maddy.

"See each other?" Maddy shot back. "I'm in a relationship with someone. I don't want to be seeing anyone else."

"Oh...Do you love her?"

"Yes." Maddy couldn't believe how good it felt to say that. "I'm not interested in having an affair with you."

"No one would have to know." Christine stepped closer and touched Maddy's arm. "Come on, Maddy. Take a chance."

Christine's perfume stirred warm recollections of the nights they had spent together. Maddy sighed and stepped back. "Christine, please stop. You're deluding yourself."

"It could be good again."

"No. No, it can't."

"It's that woman I saw working here, isn't it? The one whose kid is in your class."

"It doesn't matter who it is. You should leave, now."

"God, I can't believe you want this to be goodbye." Christine reached both hands up and cupped Maddy's face. "I was a fool. I'm sorry."

TERESA TURNED INTO Maddy's driveway and felt a chill run through her when she saw Christine's car. She slowed to a stop behind Maddy's car and stepped out. She trusted Maddy, but she knew that Christine was still hoping to patch things up. Why was Christine meeting Maddy at her apartment? Surely, Maddy hadn't invited her over.

Teresa walked across the yard. She caught movement out of the corner of her eye and stood rooted in place as she absorbed the intimate interaction between Maddy and Christine down by the pond. She could hear their voices, but the words were lost on the wind.

Startled by Christine's hands cupping her face, Maddy went still and didn't react the instant that Christine kissed her. Maddy experienced a tumult of emotions before she found the means to put her hands on Christine's shoulders and gently push her away. Christine held onto Maddy's hands, tears brimming in her eyes.

"I love you, Maddy."

"I'm sorry, Christine," Maddy said gently. "You have to believe me. It's over, finished between us."

Something twisted inside Teresa as she watched. She stood rooted in utter disbelief. Was this really happening? She felt like a fool standing there watching them. She wished this were a bad dream, but she knew it wasn't.

As she tried to decide what to do, Maddy stepped back, and for a split second, Teresa saw the look of shock and dismay register on her face when their eyes finally met. Suddenly, Teresa wanted to be anywhere but standing right here in Maddy's yard. Tears stung her eyes as she fumbled with the keys to the door, and she practically ran inside. She actually felt nauseous as she climbed the stairs.

She fought back bouts of tears, and her hands trembled as she started to gather her tools. She'd been foolish to get involved with someone again. She was desperate to get herself under control and get out of there before Maddy found her.

Teresa heard the door opening below and footsteps coming slowly up the stairs. She wiped her eyes, furious at herself for crying.

"Teresa?" Maddy stood in the doorway, looking at her. Maddy could sense Teresa's tension from across the room.

Teresa stood in the center of the half-spackled bedroom,

feeling unexpectedly awkward and foolish. She felt as though someone had punched her in the gut and all the air had rushed out of her lungs.

"I didn't know you were here." Maddy instantly regretted the words as she slowly walked toward Teresa.

"Of course, you didn't," Teresa snapped, suddenly angry and jealous.

For a moment, Maddy was taken aback, but then she said, "I think we need to talk about it."

"Tell me what we need to talk about, Maddy." Teresa knew they were heading for an argument. There was no way to prevent it. Her emotions were like a raging river overflowing its rain-swollen banks.

"We need to talk about what you saw happening out back," Maddy said gently.

Teresa nodded, determined not to cry. "I saw you kissing her."

"Yes, you did."

"At least, you're honest enough to admit it," Teresa replied curtly.

The bitter words stung and something hot and sharp like panic filled Maddy's gut. "Please, let me explain."

"Explain? What the hell is there to explain?" Teresa shouted, losing control and realizing almost instantly how fragile her hold on it had been. "Do you still have feelings for her?"

"I was telling Christine goodbye." Maddy started forward, then stopped. "And she kissed me."

Teresa didn't want to hear it. She felt betrayed, and all the old wounds from Erin's betrayal came rushing back in a torrent of emotion. She turned away, unwilling to look at Maddy anymore.

"You didn't answer my question. Do you still have feelings for her?"

"We spent almost seven years together, Teresa. I have feelings for her, but not the kind you're implying."

"How am I supposed to trust that what we shared the past few weeks was real?"

"I know it was real because right now, standing here, I feel like my heart is breaking." Maddy's heart sank as she looked across the room at the rigid set of Teresa's shoulders. "You have to believe that there's nothing left for Christine and me. It's been over for a long time."

"If you were in my position, wouldn't what I just saw bother you?"

"Yes. Yes, of course it would bother me," Maddy said miserably.

Teresa picked up her tool belt, draped it over her shoulder, and walked past Maddy.

Maddy stepped forward and touched Teresa's arm. "Wait...Teresa. Please don't leave like this."

Teresa stopped and stole a glance over her shoulder, actually looking at Maddy's face. "Why? So you can continue to justify it to me?"

Shaking inside, Maddy watched Teresa walk toward the door. "Please, don't do this. I don't love Christine." As she said it, tears rolled down her cheeks.

Questions and doubts raged through Teresa as she hurried down the stairs and out the front door. Frayed and worn out, she hardly noticed that Christine's car was gone until she got to her truck.

When she opened the door, she saw the paint chips on the seat and stared at them for a second. Angrily, she knocked them to the floor and climbed in. Right now, she needed to get away from Maddy and figure things out for herself.

THE NEXT FEW days were hell for Teresa. She tried not to think about Maddy but working on her house made that virtually impossible. She made sure she didn't run into Maddy and even avoided her when she picked Brian up at school. She cried at the strangest times and felt herself slipping back into the depression she had fought so hard to get past. She tried to rationalize that she hadn't spent enough time with Maddy to fall for her, only a month, but her heart told her that wasn't true.

By early Friday afternoon, Teresa was finishing up the last of the spackling when she heard tires crunching on the gravel outside. Her heart leapt into her throat when she thought it might be Maddy.

She peered out the second-floor window and was relieved and a little confused to see that it was Betty. Teresa met her as she was coming in the door. "I thought you were at work today. What's up? Is Rich okay?"

Betty was wearing faded jeans, a pink turtleneck, and a well-worn leather jacket that had seen better days.

"He's doing fine." She reached out and grasped Teresa's hand. "I wanted to see if you were okay."

"Me? I'm fine."

"Funny, Maddy said the same thing to me yesterday, and yet, she looks as though she lost her best friend. You don't have to tell me if you don't want to, but I can tell by looking at you that something's wrong."

Teresa's shoulders sagged. "I don't want to bore you with the details."

"What are friends for? I don't mind listening, and besides, you look like you could use someone to talk to. How does the Casa Maya sound?"

"Now?"

"Why not?"

If anything, dinner at the Casa Maya sounded good to Teresa, and she looked forward to the distraction.

INSIDE THE BRIGHTLY decorated restaurant, Teresa and Betty sat in a corner booth. After a brief look at the menu, Teresa ordered a combination special and an iced tea. Betty ordered a vegetarian bean dish and water.

"Are you doing the diet with Rich?"

"I don't want him to do it alone. Besides, it's not so bad. I've lost ten pounds, and I feel like I have more energy."

"That's fantastic."

"Yeah." Betty sipped her water as the waiter set Teresa's iced tea on the table. "So, do you want to tell me why you look as though you lost your best friend, too, or do I have to piece the clues together myself?"

Teresa picked up her drink and took a healthy sip from it. "It just sucks."

"What? Maddy didn't like the trim she picked out, the light fixtures... come on here, I've been listening to Rich tell me something's wrong for two days, but he has no clue what it is."

"It's none of that," Teresa said, slowly. "Did Rich tell you about the blonde who drove up in that smart-looking BMW a few weeks ago?"

"The babe he described as trouble?"

"That's the one. She showed up on Tuesday, and well, I wish I hadn't been there to see what I did."

"Tell me what happened."

Teresa quietly recounted the events of Tuesday in a detached, unemotional voice. Her tone belied the turmoil of emotions that were still raw inside.

"That must have been unpleasant."

"It was. I felt like an idiot. I had just come back from town, and the two of them are standing back by Maddy's pond in the middle of this kiss. I didn't know what to do, and then Maddy looks up and sees me. I know the true meaning of a 'deer in the headlights' look."

A smile flitted across Betty's lips as she sat back and twirled her knife slowly. "Besides this kiss that you saw, do you think anything else went on?"

"I have no idea, and frankly, I don't care." Teresa looked up as the waiter set their plates down.

"Do you know what the deal is with the ex-girlfriend?"

"She swears it's over between them." Teresa set her arms on the table and shook her head. "Dammit, Betty, I'm too old for this bullshit."

Betty speared a slice of avocado. "Do you trust her?"

Teresa shrugged. "I did. I guess I do."

"Well, before you write her off, at least give Maddy the opportunity to explain what happened, and then make a decision."

"We've already talked about it. There's nothing else to say."

"You talked about it in the heat of the moment. Now you've had a couple of days to let your blood simmer down and evaluate the situation with a clear mind."

"You just think I've cooled down." Teresa closed her eyes. "Evaluate. You sound like such a teacher."

"It's hard to get away from it after twenty-five years."

"This is such a mess."

"Only if you let it continue to be one." Betty leaned forward and touched Teresa's hand. "Listen, Rich and I broke up two times before we finally got hitched."

"I never knew that."

"The first time was when an old boyfriend of mine showed up at a bar. I had a couple of drinks in me and gave him a hug and a kiss right in front of Rich. Of course, we got into a terrible argument, and he broke up with me that night. We got back together a few months later, and then one of Rich's old flames showed up, and he decided that he wanted us to cool things for a while. I guess what I'm trying to say, Teresa, is none of us is perfect, and we all make mistakes."

"Jealousy is an ugly emotion, Betty."

"Yes, it is. So you saw them kissing. You really can't forgive her for something like that?"

"Betty, I'm not the one with the ex-girlfriend still lurking in the wings."

"No, but that may not be all Maddy's fault. You don't know that piece of the story. I know you have to make your own decision, but Maddy seems to be a remarkable woman. You have some things in common with each other, and you know she's crazy about Brian. We all make mistakes, and occasionally, we need someone to give us a break. Love is about compromise, Teresa. It's all about give and take and putting up with each other's shortcomings." Betty fell silent. She knew the last few years had taken their toll on Teresa and left her soul bruised and battered.

Teresa's eyes misted with tears as she looked away from Betty.

"It's only been a month. It's not as if we really know each other that well. It might be better to just let it go."

Betty poked her fork at Teresa. "Don't you say that now. Teresa Ann Parker, the last month is the happiest I have seen you in almost three years. Don't you think you both deserve another chance at love?"

"I don't want to get hurt."

Betty reached out and touched Teresa's hand. "Teresa, life is about getting knocked down and pulling yourself back up. God knows you've lived through hell. It's a whole lot easier to get back up if you have someone by your side who loves you."

"Maybe you're right, but what about Brian? I can't let him get hurt again."

"What does that teach him? Sure, you might get your heart broken, but if you don't take a risk, you'll never know. Is that what you want for yourself or for Brian, to go through life and be afraid to take a chance because he might get hurt? That's an awfully lonely way to live."

"I know it is. I felt like such a fool standing there."

"I suspect Maddy did, too," Betty said. "None of us gets through life unscathed. Whether it's an overbearing parent, an alcoholic in the family, someone who suffered emotional or physical abuse, or the death of someone we love, we've all been touched in some way, and it shapes our behavior and our responses. I can't tell you how proud I am of you. You took risks I never would have dreamed of taking had I been in your situation. I know how hard you work, and I've wondered if you ever took the time to think about what you wanted for yourself."

Teresa had never heard Betty speak this way about her, and she was touched. "I didn't for a long time. I made the changes that I needed to and did the best I could to hold it together for Brian."

"That's what we all do. The best we can do. Maybe that's what Maddy did."

Teresa sat back and rested her hands on the tablecloth. She hadn't considered that viewpoint about Maddy's actions, and it made her pause. "I'll think about what you said, Betty." She was exhausted from the conversation and relieved when they progressed to other subjects.

After they paid for dinner, Betty and Teresa walked out to their respective trucks. She thought about Rich and Betty, and the life they were building together. She had tried once before and thought she was building a life with Erin. She had been wrong, and that had only reinforced her loneliness and fear. "Thanks for listening, Betty."

"Anytime. I hope it helped."

"You gave me some things to think about."

Teresa still felt terrible as she drove home. As she thought about Maddy, she fought back tears several times.

She thought about her own life. She loved using her hands, and building houses made her feel as if she was accomplishing something. She liked the physical and mental challenges that came with the varied projects. Of course, the physical challenges would eventually make her leave that side of the business.

Her personal life was a mess. Her broken relationship with Erin had made her feel like a failure, and she didn't trust her instincts with relationships anymore. There were so many risks. Sure, it was fun and passionate in the beginning, but what happened after that? What if they fell out of love or something worse happened? She wasn't sure she could handle that roller coaster ride again.

"HOW WAS HE, Rose?" Teresa asked her neighbor when she arrived home.

"Brian was fine. We watched some television. He got sleepy trying to wait up for you and went to bed."

Teresa walked Rose to the door. "Thanks, and let me know when you want me to fix that screen door for you."

"There's no rush. Whenever you have time, Teresa. Goodnight."

Teresa waited until Rose pulled out of the driveway before she closed and locked the front door.

Brian was sleeping soundly. Teresa kissed him lightly on his temple and went into her own bedroom.

As she changed into a nightshirt and climbed between the sheets, she thought about Maddy. Less than a week ago, she had been lying in bed with Maddy snuggled up beside her. They'd spent a day with Brian, Rich, and Betty, and before that evening was over, Teresa allowed herself to fantasize about Maddy as part of their family.

Maybe she'd been a fool all along to think that Maddy was over her ex-lover.

Forcing Maddy out of her mind, Teresa turned off the light. From now on, she needed to concentrate solely on herself and Brian. Their brief affair was finished. It needed to be shoved into a dark corner of her mind where it couldn't come back to haunt her.

Chapter
Seventeen

MADDY KNEW THERE was trouble the minute she heard shrill voices coming from behind the slide on the playground. She heard Brian's voice first followed by another boy's, and she started in their direction.

"They're in heaven."

"Maybe they aren't. My father said if you can't see something then it's just a fairy tale."

"But heaven is there," Brian said with an absoluteness to his voice.

"That's just a stupid fairy tale."

"No, it isn't."

Maddy turned the corner in time to see him push Teddy hard in the chest.

"You're a baby because you believe in fairy tales." Teddy regained his footing and kicked Brian in the knee. "Brian's a baby."

"No, I'm not."

"Both of you stop, right now." Maddy got between the two boys and held them apart with her arms.

"He pushed me first," Teddy said, and stuck his tongue out at Brian.

One look at Brian and Maddy knew he was about to cry. "I don't care who started it. We do not hit or kick in this school. Do you both understand?"

The boys nodded silently.

Maddy took Teddy by the shoulders and squatted down in front of him. "Teddy, it's not nice to make fun of what other people believe in."

Teddy furrowed his eyebrows and looked away. "But my father says heaven is a fairy tale."

"Just because your father says that doesn't mean it's right to make someone feel bad for what he believes in. Do you understand?"

"Yes, Ms. Geddes."

"Now, I need the two of you to say you're sorry to each other."

"Sorry, Brian."

Maddy looked over her shoulder at Brian.

"Sorry I pushed you," he said.

"Teddy, go tell the boys playing kickball it's almost time to go in."

Maddy stood up and walked back to Brian. "Are you all right?"

He nodded but big tears rolled down his face and his chest heaved as he held in a sob.

"Come on. Let's go inside." She took his hand and walked with him across the parking lot. She stopped and spoke briefly with one of the other teachers who quickly agreed to bring Maddy's class inside at the end of recess.

She took Brian to the nurse's office. It was quiet there, and he could gather himself without being embarrassed to cry in front of his classmates. She sat beside him in one of the chairs and watched as he pulled one knee up close and rested his chin on it.

"Do you want to talk about what happened?"

Brian rubbed his eyes and shook his head. "No. I want to go home."

Maddy looked up as the school nurse walked into the office. "Hi, Tina."

"What happened, Brian?" Tina asked in a cheerful tone as she bent down in front of him.

When Brian didn't answer, Maddy motioned Tina to follow her. In the hallway, Maddy gave her a quick rundown on what had happened out on the playground.

"What do you want me to do, Maddy?"

Maddy considered this for a moment. "Give him some time, and see if he'll come back to my class. If not, call his aunt so she can pick him up. We need to let her know what happened anyway."

"All right. I'll do that."

"Thanks, Tina."

Maddy stepped through the doorway. "Brian, I have to go back to the classroom. You can stay here with Nurse Tina for a while."

Brian looked up at her through tearful eyes. "Is Teddy right about heaven, Ms. Geddes?"

Maddy's mind scrambled for an answer. "I don't think so, Brian. I believe in heaven, too."

He seemed to look right through Maddy, and then he turned his gaze back to staring at the wall.

Maddy shared a concerned glance with Tina as she walked past her.

TERESA DROVE TO the elementary school with her eyes on the road and her mind on Brian. She couldn't imagine what happened at school that the nurse would call and leave a cryptic message on her cell phone. Her stomach knotted as she replayed the message in her mind.

"Hi, Ms. Parker. This is Tina the nurse at Brian's school. It's not an emergency, but I do need to speak to you about what happened today on the playground before you pick Brian up from school."

When Teresa arrived at the school, she got out of her truck and walked inside to the office. She stopped at the doorway, waiting until the secretary finished her conversation and hung up the phone.

"Can I help you?" The woman pushed her glasses up on her nose

"Hi, I'm Brian Parker's aunt. The nurse called and asked me to speak with her before I pick up Brian."

The woman's expression changed to one of displeasure. "Nurse Tina had an emergency, and she had to leave early. She was hoping you would be here before the end of the day to pick Brian up."

"She didn't say that I needed to come and pick him up early, and I do work full time. Where can I find Brian?"

"You'll have to go to his classroom."

"Thank you," Teresa said, with a clipped tone to her voice.

She found Brian sitting with Maddy in the classroom at the end of the hallway. His legs were swinging from the chair and crayons were scattered on the teacher's desk in front of him. Maddy's back was to the door, but Teresa could see that she was leaning toward Brian with her elbow resting on the desk.

They didn't notice her standing in the doorway, and she heard Brian speak to Maddy as he colored.

"Do you think there are clouds in heaven, Ms. Geddes?"

"I think there are big fluffy clouds the angels lie on while they look down at earth."

"Do you think my mom and dad miss me?"

"I imagine they do, Brian." Maddy must have sensed Teresa's presence because she turned, and her smile faded when she saw Teresa standing there watching them. "Hello, Teresa."

Teresa acknowledged Maddy with a nod of her head and walked over to Brian.

"What are you working on?" Teresa looked at the array of drawings on the desk. She was surprised at what she saw. One drawing showed a black and green monster chasing a wild-eyed stick figure. Brian handed Teresa the piece of blue construction paper filled with white blobs she assumed were clouds. Scribbled in the middle of the page was a small circle of blue and green.

"Heaven," Brian said matter-of-factly, as he clutched a white crayon.

Teresa pulled a chair over and sat slightly behind Brian, keeping her distance from Maddy.

"What happened today?"

Teresa waited as Brian took another piece of paper and drew a monster biting off the head of a helpless victim. He colored blobs of red at the stick figure's feet.

"Teddy said heaven was a fairy tale for babies."

"What did you say?" Teresa's gaze briefly contacted Maddy's. The pictures made sense to her now. Teddy was the boy in the picture, and the monster was Brian's way of exacting his revenge.

"I told him he was wrong. There is a heaven. Right, Ms. Geddes?"

"Yes, there is, Brian," Maddy said softly, not entirely trusting her voice.

"I'm sorry he said that to you." Teresa leaned in, kissed his cheek, and squeezed his shoulders in a comforting hug.

Brian nodded and kept coloring.

"Brian, I'm going to talk to Ms. Geddes. We'll be right back." Teresa stood and walked to the hallway out of earshot from him.

Maddy could sense the change in Teresa as she followed her into the hall.

"The nurse called and wanted to speak to me, but she's left for the day. Do you know what she wanted to see me about?" Teresa barely looked at Maddy as she spoke.

It took all Maddy's effort to hold her feelings in check. "I asked her to call you. As calm as Brian is now, I think you can imagine how upset he was earlier by what the other boy said to him."

"Kids can be so damn cruel to each other." Teresa took a deep breath and let it out as she looked into the classroom at Brian still coloring. "Thank you."

"For what?" Maddy said, struggling with the strange sensation of standing so close to the woman she'd fallen in love with and feeling as if Teresa had shut herself off to her emotionally since Tuesday.

"For watching over Brian." The silence grew between them, and Teresa made a move to walk away.

"Teresa, can I ask you something?" Maddy reached out to touch her arm.

Teresa nodded, unable to meet Maddy's gaze.

"Can we please talk? I can't continue this way not knowing what you're thinking."

"I don't have an answer for you."

"How can you say that?" Maddy asked, with a hint of sadness and resignation creeping into her voice.

"Because I don't have an answer," Teresa said in a harsh tone, refusing to be pushed farther on the topic. "I'm going to take Brian home now."

Maddy stepped aside, fighting the ache that started in her throat. Teresa walked over to Brian and squatted down beside him. Maddy couldn't hear what she said, but Brian quickly climbed out of the chair and wrapped his arms and legs around Teresa. With some effort, Teresa stood up, squeezed him tightly to her, and gathered the pictures from the desk.

Maddy could see tears in Teresa's eyes as she carried Brian toward the door, rubbing his back in a gentle circular motion and whispering in his ear. The embrace was a maternal display of love that touched Maddy deeply. Without thinking, she reached out toward Brian's outstretched hand, and he clutched at her.

"Bye, Ms. Geddes."

"Bye, Brian." Maddy let his hand go and fought back the tears that welled in her eyes as Teresa walked down the hallway away from her.

At the bottom of the steps, Teresa set Brian down and held his hand. It had been a long time since he had needed to be carried or held, and she was surprised when he gripped her hand tightly.

"Teresa?"

"What Brian?"

"I think Ms. Geddes was sad today."

Teresa glanced down at Brian as he stopped walking and looked up at her. "Why do you say that?"

"I saw her crying when we left."

"I should call you eagle eyes."

"Why?"

"You notice everything."

"Oh. You're sad, too."

"I'm sad because that boy made you feel bad today." Teresa needed to make Brian understand her own tears were for him and no other reason. He saw more than some adults would see.

"You should talk to Ms. Geddes, Teresa."

"Why?"

"Because you're her friend. Friends look out for each other. That's what friends do, right?"

"Yeah, that's what friends do," Teresa said quietly as they headed outside.

Chapter
Eighteen

MADDY CARRIED A flashlight and roamed aimlessly through the construction site looking at all the work that was done. She could tell Teresa had been working here during the week when she had been at school teaching. The thought made her sad and angry at the same time. All the spackling and sanding was finished. As far as she could tell, only the molding needed to be installed.

When she had returned home Friday afternoon, she found pieces of wood and some handles in a plastic bag tied around her apartment doorknob. A note was taped to the door.

Here are two molding samples and handles that would work with the architecture of the house. Let Rich know which ones you decide on.

Teresa

The scrawled note was a bitter reminder of Tuesday's events. Maddy was still reeling from what happened with Christine. She thought she had handled everything well, telling Christine in no uncertain terms that she didn't want a relationship, but then Christine had kissed her.

It wasn't that she had responded to it; she had pushed Christine away, and that would have been fine except Teresa had witnessed the whole thing.

Maddy carefully descended the stairs, closed the door behind her, and locked it. With her arms wrapped tightly across her chest to ward off the evening chill, she walked across the yard to her apartment.

All afternoon, she had vacillated through a range of emotions from anger to frustration, from worry to exasperation, only to start over again. So many thoughts were rushing through her mind, she had a hard time sorting them out.

Teresa had been so hurt and angry. Part of Maddy couldn't

blame her, but another side was cross that Teresa wouldn't stay to hear her out.

Maddy tried turning on the television to distract her, but it was no use. Her mind wouldn't let go of the memories, so she turned the TV off and went to bed. But she kept hearing Teresa's voice.

"I just kept building one project after another. I worked, Brian went to school, and another year went by. This spring came, and I saw the buds form on the trees while we laid the foundation for your house. I smelled the rain and the grass and heard the birds singing for the first time in a long while. I met you and here we are."

Maddy couldn't sleep that night. Was she really going to lose Teresa over an unwelcome kiss?

As she lay thinking, she recalled the evening they spent together barely a week ago and how Teresa made love to her right here in this bed. She remembered the expression on Teresa's face as she listened to her talk and how it made her feel to know that Teresa was interested in her as a person.

Maddy wished she had summoned the courage to tell Teresa she loved her as they lay in each other's arms after making love. They had talked softly to each other long into the night. She'd felt peace in Teresa's embrace.

It had felt right, almost perfect, as if they were destined to meet.

She could imagine Brian and Teresa here in her new home celebrating Christmas and opening gifts. The picture of the three of them sitting around the Christmas tree came unbidden, and Maddy felt a hot pang of grief at the possibility of that never happening.

The sadness was so strong that it astounded her. She rolled over, clutching her pillow tightly as hot tears rolled down her cheeks. She didn't think she could live in the same town and see Brian everyday at school with the way things were. It would hurt too much.

"MADDY, IT'S ME!" Angela let herself in the door to Maddy's apartment.

She'd been worried since Friday night when two phone calls were unanswered and her messages went unreturned. Even though Maddy was careful, it concerned Angela that so many contractors were in and out of the house.

"Maddy?"

"I'm in the bedroom." Maddy sat up in bed and blinked as she read the time on the clock. It was nine o'clock in the morning.

"Are you sick?"

"No."

"Then why haven't you called me back?"

Maddy shoved the covers aside and swung her legs over the edge of the bed. "My heart is sick."

"What? What happened?"

Maddy let her head fall forward and sighed. "Christine showed up here on Tuesday. She's been trying to get back together with me since her girlfriend broke up with her."

"What a pig she is."

"I guess Tuesday was her last-ditch effort after she sent the roses to school on Monday."

"So what happened?"

"We talked out in the back by the pond. I told her it was over, and then she grabbed hold of my face and kissed me. She totally caught me off guard, and I didn't react right away."

"And?"

"Teresa saw it happen."

"Oh, Maddy. Don't think for one minute that Christine didn't plan and hope she would screw something up for you. God, she is so transparent. The only time she's okay with herself is when everyone else around her is miserable." Angela sat down on the bed. "What did Teresa say?"

"She was hurt and angry. I tried to explain, but she didn't want to hear it."

"Today's Saturday. Have you called her?"

"I don't know what to say."

Angela stood up and eyed Maddy. "First, go take a shower and get dressed. Then we'll plan your strategy."

It didn't take long for Maddy to shower and change into a pair of jeans and a white pullover shirt. When she walked into the kitchen, she breathed in the aroma of coffee brewing.

"That smells wonderful."

Angela handed Maddy a mug of the steaming beverage. "Sit and listen to me. First, you need to go talk to Teresa today. The longer you don't talk, the worse this is going to get."

"But what do I say? I kissed Christine and Teresa saw it happen. Nothing's going to change that."

"No, but how do you feel about Teresa?"

"I don't want to lose her."

"I didn't ask that. How do you feel about her?"

"I love her."

"Then this is what you need to do..."

"ARE YOU SURE this will work?" Maddy asked twenty minutes later.

Angela tilted her head and smiled. "What I know is that if you do nothing now, more time is going to pass, and it will be easier for Teresa to walk away from you without ever knowing if what you two have right now is worth fighting for."

MADDY DIDN'T CALL Teresa before she left her house Saturday morning. She wanted the opportunity to talk face to face, and she was afraid Teresa might refuse. On the drive over, Maddy rehearsed exactly what she wanted to say. She had to tell Teresa she loved her. It might be the only thing she could do to salvage their relationship.

She heard the rumble of a lawnmower as she pulled up in front of Teresa's house and parked on the street. She didn't see Brian outside and wondered whether he was inside or visiting a friend.

She walked around the side of the house and noticed that Teresa had pruned every shrub since the last time Maddy had been here. She paused at the corner and collected herself before moving around to the back where the lawnmower sounded louder.

Teresa was pushing the lawnmower up a slight hill, and her face was flushed from the heat and exertion.

Maddy walked across the yard and called out. "Hey." She waved her hand to get Teresa's attention as she turned the lawnmower around to start back in the opposite direction.

Teresa stared at her blankly and relaxed her hand on the throttle, allowing the engine to cut out.

"Hi," she said, standing with the lawnmower between them. She deliberately hadn't contacted Maddy since she saw her at school on Wednesday. "You caught me getting some chores done while Brian's over at one of his friends."

"That's what weekends are for, catching up on chores."

"Yeah, I suppose. If I did some during the week, it wouldn't all end up being done on the weekend." Instead of walking toward Maddy, Teresa bent over and removed the grass catcher from the back of the lawnmower.

"It happens to all of us. We're so busy during the week."

"Did you pick out the molding you want installed?" Teresa's voice sounded flat.

Maddy stepped closer and ended the small talk. "I did, but that's not why I'm here."

Teresa wasn't sure what emotion she had expected to feel when she saw Maddy, but sadness and regret was what settled deep in her heart. She glanced at Maddy, standing there in jeans and a simple white shirt, and then she carried the bag of grass toward the back of her property.

"What's going on with us?" Maddy said.

Teresa shook the bag, emptying the grass into a pile on the ground. "Nothing."

Maddy stared at her through a frozen haze of anguish. "How can you say nothing? We haven't talked since Wednesday."

Teresa stopped shaking the bag and looked over at Maddy, meeting her gaze directly for the first time. Maddy could sense Teresa's growing anger. "I don't know what else you want me to say. You didn't even tell me you were sorry that you kissed her, damn it. So, why don't you give me a break?"

The venom in Teresa's voice stunned Maddy, and she stumbled clumsily over her words. "I...yes, I am sorry. I didn't want her to kiss me. She just did."

Teresa walked back to the lawnmower and reattached the bag. "I guess it was inconvenient that I showed up at that time."

This was going very badly, Maddy decided. "I don't want to fight with you."

"I don't, either."

"Teresa, it was a stupid kiss that didn't mean anything other than goodbye. I'm sorry you're upset. If I could do it over, I would have handled it differently, but I can't." Maddy's shoulders drooped. She was losing Teresa. "You have to know I would never do anything to hurt you or Brian."

Teresa's head jerked up at the mention of Brian's name. "I made a promise to my brother to take care of Brian."

"I know that."

"In the past month, he's spent more time with Rich and Betty than he has since he's lived with me."

"I didn't think that was a bad thing."

"I didn't, either, until Tuesday. That's when it hit me that I've been with you more than I have with him. What a waste of time."

"Teresa, please don't be like this."

"Be like what? Brian has to be my priority, not chasing a shadow of something that might be."

"What does that mean for us?" Maddy felt tears begin to well in her eyes.

"It's better we end this now, before things get more complicated." Teresa looked away, unable to bear the pain in Maddy's eyes.

"More complicated?"

"Yes." Teresa walked past Maddy, heading to the back door.

Maddy marched after her and grasped her arm gently. "I'm not going to let you walk away from what we have."

Teresa looked at Maddy out of the corner of her eye. "What we had." Her voice faded, and she turned away to open the door and keep her face from betraying her emotions.

As Teresa let the door go, Maddy caught it and followed her inside. "Don't walk away from me, and don't dismiss me."

Teresa washed her hands in the sink and said in a resigned voice, "Look, I've said what I need to say."

"Well, I've got some things to say to you, Teresa Parker. What we had together was more than just a fling." Maddy's voice started to break, and she pressed her lips together to control it. "It was more than that, and I know you felt it, too."

Teresa sat down at the kitchen table, so there was physical distance between them. Part of her wanted to curl up in the dark somewhere and go to sleep, where none of this mattered.

"You shrugged me off on Wednesday," Maddy said. "I didn't appreciate it."

Teresa stared at her blankly. "I had a right to be upset."

"I'm not saying you didn't. You see, the problem was I told myself I wasn't ready to fall in love again. But I didn't realize I wouldn't have a choice about it."

Teresa pulled one knee up to her chest and rested her chin on it as tears brimmed in her eyes. When Maddy started toward her, she shook her head and waved her hand for Maddy to keep away. "No, don't. I was so hurt when I saw you and Christine kissing. Then I was scared that I had already lost you. Feeling that way pissed me off." She looked up through the blur of tears and saw Maddy was crying too.

Teresa rubbed the wetness from her face. "Even when I was mad, I couldn't figure out why you would have done so much to help Brian and gotten involved with me just to turn around and throw it all away."

"That's just it. I wouldn't do that. Something about Brian touched me when I met him. You and Brian have made me feel as though I'm part of a family. I never felt that way with anyone else."

"Then I'd say you haven't been with the right person." Teresa stood up and got tissues for both of them. She handed one to Maddy but still kept her distance.

"You were the only one," Teresa said, "except for Rich and Betty, who ever acknowledged I lost my brother when the accident happened. Maybe it's selfish to feel that way, but even with Erin, in her own warped way, it was all about Brian, like my loss didn't count."

Maddy wiped her eyes and blew her nose. "Why is it we never seem to know the person we're with until something bad happens?"

"Because trauma strips away the defenses, and we see someone's true nature in that situation. In any case, it's just a

snapshot of that moment. It's not who she is as a human being."
Teresa walked over and brushed a tear away from Maddy's cheek
with her thumb. "I care about you, Maddy."

"I don't want to lose you, Teresa." Maddy grasped her hand
before she could step away.

"Tell me the truth," Teresa said. "Are you falling in love with
me?"

There was a crack in Teresa's voice, and Maddy spoke calmly.
"It feels as if I am."

"I don't know if I'm ready for that," Teresa admitted quietly.

"I'm not asking for you to tell me you love me. We'll take
things one day at a time. I'm tired of feeling alone and letting the
days just pass me by. When I'm with you, I don't feel that way."

"You need to know," Teresa said, "there are still days when I
feel as though the bad memories are sucking me down, and it's all I
can do to get out of bed."

"But you still get up and help Brian get through everyday. I
admire that. It takes a lot of courage."

"It's not courage. It's looking into Brian's eyes and knowing
I'm all he has to depend on."

Maddy moved closer and cupped Teresa's face in her hands.
"You are Brian's compass, his true north, his hero."

"Don't put that on me." Teresa's eyes filled again with tears,
and she closed them tightly. She lowered her head against Maddy's
shoulder, but the dam had already broken. "You had to go and get
me crying. You had my heart the first night we kissed, Madeline
Geddes. It felt as if it got ripped out when I saw you on Tuesday."

Maddy let Teresa step back. "I'm so sorry. I didn't mean for
you to get hurt or have you believe I was having second thoughts
about us."

Teresa plopped down in the chair as her stomach did flip-
flops. "You're stubborn as hell, aren't you?"

"When it comes to things I consider worth fighting for, I am."

Teresa brushed the tears from her eyes and looked up at the
clock on the kitchen wall. It was one o'clock. "I have to pick up
Brian."

"Would it be too forward of me to ask if I can come along?"

"I think it would make Brian very happy to see you."

Chapter
Nineteen

THE FOLLOWING WEEK, TERESA SPENT MOST of her time cutting and installing the molding in the rooms of Maddy's new house. She was pushing hard to get the job done because Rich had two new projects lined up to start in October. The goal was to get them framed and closed in before the bad weather slowed them down.

Teresa was proud of the work she'd done. The covered front porch had delicate wooden posts anchored on stone bases, and other craftsman accents were evident throughout the design of the house. Her favorite room was the living room. Its eastern-facing bay window let the morning sun bathe the room with light, and the rustic stone fireplace dominated the opposite wall.

She was working in that room now. The high-pitched whine of the miter saw faded, and she stepped back to inspect the angle of the cut. She was just about to climb the ladder with the mitred piece when she heard heavy footsteps approaching from the hallway. Rich walked into the room, his boots leaving impressions in the sawdust behind him.

"Aren't you going to pick up Brian?" he said.

"I want to get this last piece up, and then I'm leaving."

"Oh, usually you've already left by now." He sounded surprised and continued to stand inside the doorway watching her work. Teresa was glad he hadn't been asking any questions about what happened between her and Maddy.

"He gets tutored on Mondays. He won't mind spending a few minutes extra with Maddy anyway. He likes hanging out with her. I'll get this room finished, and then I'll start the trim in the bathroom after we eat dinner."

Rich took a step forward and said, "So, things are working out between you two?"

"Yeah." Teresa looked at him with a slightly embarrassed grin on her face. "We're taking it a day at a time."

"How's Brian feeling about everything?"

"Okay. I really haven't talked to him about *us* yet. I wanted some more time to see how things are going before we have that conversation."

Rich laughed and rocked back on his feet. "The boy's no dummy, Teresa. He can see the stars in your eyes just as well as the next person."

"I guess he can, but I'll know when the time is right."

"I know you will. I'm just teasing you. So how's he doing in school?"

"He had a rough time last week." Teresa related the incident with one of Brian's classmates.

Rich looked dismayed. "How did Brian handle it?"

"He pushed the kid and told him he was wrong."

"Good for him."

"Then he fell apart afterward in the nurse's office."

"That's okay. He stood his ground to that bully."

"How do you know the kid's a bully?"

"Any kid who can sniff out a weakness like that and exploit it just for the sake of causing someone harm is a bully in my book. That's shitty timing with the anniversary of the accident coming up this week."

"Yeah, it is."

Teresa dreaded the arrival of that day on so many emotional levels. She could feel it coming like the ominous rumble of a freight train. The closer the anniversary got, the more she shut down, not allowing herself to feel or think about the memories of that day. To do so was overwhelming. Innumerable times over the past three years, she had wept raw, anguished tears that left her shaken and weary.

They had made it through all the firsts. The first Christmas, the first birthdays, and the first anniversary. This year, like the last two, they would take flowers to the cemetery to set on the gravesite, maybe take a walk in the park, and then they would go to the church to light a candle for David and Fran.

"I know it's a tough day for you and Brian."

"I used to wonder if it would ever get easier to deal with."

"Has it?" Rich stuck his hands in his pockets and waited for her response.

"It's different. The grief's still there, but it's not as edgy and sharp. There are still days when it catches me by surprise, and I find myself crying unexpectedly. I guess what I wish for most is that Brian grows up to be all right."

"He will."

"How do you know that?" Teresa's voice cracked, and she pressed her lips together.

"Because I remember the promise you made David at the funeral."

Tears started to roll down Teresa's cheeks, and she allowed Rich to pull her into a hug. He repeated from memory the words she uttered standing in front of David and Fran's coffins at the church. "I promise you both I will take care of Brian all the days of my life. I promise to teach him values, so he knows the difference between right from wrong. I will be there to support him in his disappointments and share in his joys. I'll love him as if he were my own."

"Jesus, you remembered that?" Embarrassed at herself for crying, Teresa hastily wiped the tears from her face.

"I think those words were tattooed on my heart that day. Listen, maybe after you and Brian finish at the church you can come by and we'll have dinner. What do you say?"

After a moment's silence recalling how she and Brian had spent last year sharing a pizza alone at the end of an emotionally exhausting day, Teresa decided it was a good idea. "It'll be a nice way to end the day."

"Then it's settled. You'll come to dinner at our place."

IT WAS LATE when Brian and Teresa returned home from Maddy's house.. Teresa pulled the small stack of envelopes out of the mailbox and handed the keys to Brian, so he could unlock the front door.

"I had fun playing Crazy Eights with Ms. Geddes tonight."

"I could tell," Teresa said, with a rueful smile. She had finished putting up the bathroom trim while Maddy and Brian sat on the floor playing the card game. Listening to their laughter and Brian's protests when he lost a particularly close game drew Teresa deeper into the fantasy of the three of them being together as a family.

"Brian, it's too late to watch TV," Teresa said, when she saw Brian pick up the remote control and turn on the television.

"Oh, man..."

"Please go brush your teeth and get into your pajamas." She sorted through the mail while he stomped away. Teresa saw the envelope and stared at it for a moment before it registered why she had received a piece of mail from her attorney's office.

She opened the envelope and pulled out the heavy bond paper. In her hand she held the formal adoption papers for Brian. Seeing the words in writing was almost funny and a little anticlimactic. The entire process had taken almost two and a half years because of the custody suit filed by Brian's grandparents. The paper itself was a formality, but still, Teresa carried it to

Brian's room to show it to him.

His door was slightly ajar, and she knocked softly before she poked her head into the room. He was lying on his stomach with his chin propped on one hand as he flipped through the pages of the photo album. He looked up at Teresa a little sheepishly because he was still in his clothes.

"I just wanted to see their faces."

"I've been thinking about your mom and dad a lot this week." Teresa sat on the edge of the bed with the paper rolled loosely in the palm of her hand.

"You have?"

"The anniversary is Saturday."

"I miss them. I wish they could come back."

"I know you do." Teresa leaned back against the headboard, and Brian rested his head on her lap.

"What's that?" He pointed to the rolled up adoption decree in her hand.

Teresa handed it to him and watched as he looked at the words and read them.

"What does it mean?"

"It means that I get to raise you as if you were my own child."

"Like you told Daddy you would."

She was surprised that he had any recollection of that, but he had stood beside her and held her hand tightly when she had said those words at the church. "Yes, just like I promised your mom and dad."

"What does that make you?"

Teresa rubbed Brian's back in a circular motion as he rested on her lap. "It makes me your parent."

"What do I get to call you now?"

Teresa closed her eyes and tilted her head back. "You can still call me Aunt Teresa."

She heard his deep breaths and felt the rise and fall of his chest under her arm as he drifted off to sleep without another word. She waited a few minutes before she gingerly lifted him off her lap and settled him on the bed.

Back in the living room, she filed the adoption certificate with her other important papers about Brian.

She sat down at the small desk and rested her head in her hands. The week had begun as the second worst in her life, and it was ending up as one of the best. After she had picked up Brian and Maddy, the three of them had gone out for pizza. Throughout dinner, she was conscious of the attraction and trust she felt growing again between her and Maddy as they laughed and talked. She was also well aware that their relationship was a delicate thing that needed to be nurtured and tended to with care, for all their sakes, but especially Brian's.

Chapter
Twenty

TERESA ALWAYS LOVED autumn. Even though it signaled the end of the growing season and the days became ever shorter, she loved the clear, crisp air, and the vivid display of fall foliage.

Shortly after mid-morning on Saturday, she led Brian through the massive arched doorway of Saint Vincent's. They entered the dark interior; the only light filtered through the stained glass windows. In a small alcove, Teresa helped Brian light two candles. She said a silent prayer for Fran and David while Brian stood quietly by her side.

After a moment, Brian wrapped an arm around Teresa's waist and leaned against her.

"Are you ready to go to the cemetery?"

He nodded and together they walked from the alcove and left the church. The drive from Green Village Road to the cemetery on Noe Avenue took less than five minutes.

When they left her truck, Brian clutched her hand a little tighter as they walked along the asphalt path that led them closer to the gravesite. It had rained the night before, and drops still fell from the leaves and branches that overhung the walkway that wound through the cemetery. Birds sang overhead, and she could hear the scurrying of chipmunks and squirrels beneath the trees.

She had walked this path many times, and still as they rounded the last bend and saw the row of tombstones, she couldn't help the painful feeling that settled in her gut. God knew what it was like for Brian.

He surprised her by reaching for the tulips she held. He carried them over and set them down on the ground by the headstone. After a moment, he looked at her.

"What do you say to them, Aunt Teresa?"

Teresa closed her eyes for a second. "I tell them I love them. That I miss them, and I remember all the things we did together." She could almost hear the long ago echo of David's laughter when they were kids.

David, get down. You're going to fall.

You're just chicken, T. He laughed and climbed higher into the oak tree.

"Can I ask them a question?"

"Absolutely."

Brian squeezed his eyes shut and stood there next to Teresa, his lips moving.

She could hear most of what he whispered. "Hi, Mom. Hi, Dad. It's Brian. I love you. I miss you and wish you could come back. Mom? I have to ask you something..." His voice drifted into silence.

Several minutes later, he opened his eyes and grasped Teresa's hand. "I'm done. Can we go to Uncle Rich and Aunt Betty's now?"

"Yeah, let's go."

IT WAS JUST past noon when they got to Rich and Betty's house. Heavy rain clouds were darkening the sky, and it felt as though it was much later in the day. Teresa opened the truck door and stepped out. She walked up the steps onto the porch with Brian following her, tapped on the front door, and opened it. Betty met them just inside the kitchen.

"Aunt Betty." Brian slipped around Teresa and ran into Betty's arms.

Betty held him tightly and exchanged concerned looks with Teresa. "I love you, Brian."

"Can I go lie down on the couch?"

"Go ahead, sweetheart."

Maddy was standing behind Betty and ruffled Brian's hair as he walked to her. He stopped and gave her a hug before he stepped back and continued into the living room.

"Teresa?"

The concern in Maddy's voice almost did her in. Teresa slipped past Maddy and averted her tear-filled eyes as she tried to hide behind the safe veil of false pretense. She knew Maddy wasn't fooled. She understood the heartache of this day.

"Are you okay?"

Teresa shook her head. "No. I hate the way this day makes me feel."

The look of sad understanding in Maddy's eyes ripped away the veil. This time she couldn't stop the tears from flowing. Maddy moved toward her, took Teresa in her arms, and let her cry.

"Take a little time for yourself," Maddy said after a few minutes.

"We'll sit with Brian for a while," Betty added.

"Thanks." Teresa couldn't deny that she was barely holding herself together. She walked past the two women and stepped outside, feeling the sting of fresh tears in her eyes. She turned toward the sound of footsteps and came face to face with Rich.

He held out his arms, and she fell into them, clinging to him fiercely.

"I don't know which hurts more, missing David and Fran or hurting because of what their dying has meant for Brian."

Rich held her and let her cry.

FOR THE REST of the day, Teresa moved as though she were in a fog. Brian was clingy and shadowed her until he finally settled on the couch after dinner. She sat beside him, and he snuggled against her.

"Do you want to go home?"

He shook his head. "Stay here," he murmured, his eyes sleepy.

"We didn't bring an overnight bag for you."

"Please?"

"I'll ask Aunt Betty," Teresa whispered against his cheek.

She went to the kitchen where Rich, Maddy, and Betty were talking quietly. They looked up when she walked in.

"Brian wants to stay here tonight, Betty. Is that all right?"

"Let him," Betty said softly.

"He doesn't have any pajamas."

Betty stood. "I'm sure we have a T-shirt of his he can wear."

"I'll go say goodnight to him." Teresa returned to the living room. Brian lay curled on his side with his hands tucked underneath his cheek, fast asleep.

An ache blossomed in her chest. She knelt and caressed his cheek. She leaned in and kissed him gently. "I love you, Brian." She lingered a moment watching him before she stood up.

Out in the hallway, she hugged Rich and Betty goodnight. They were all exhausted, and it showed in their faces.

"It was good to be here with you today," Teresa said. "It was good for Brian, too."

"He'll be fine here tonight," Betty said.

"I know. Thanks for everything."

Maddy was waiting by the front door, holding Teresa's jacket. Teresa touched her cheek and felt a powerful jolt as she looked into Maddy's eyes. It came from inside, beyond the physical concrete reality of their world. It felt like coming home.

"What can I do, Teresa?"

"Take me home with you."

WHEN THEY GOT out of the car at Maddy's house, she started to say something, but Teresa didn't want to hear the words, or the burden they carried.

"Take me to bed, Maddy."

"Are you sure?"

"I don't want to think anymore. I just want to feel you."

Teresa took the keys from Maddy and unlocked the door to her apartment. Upstairs, Teresa hugged Maddy tightly, burying her face in the crook of her neck.

"Brian did okay today," Maddy said.

"He did. Can we not talk about it for tonight? I don't want to be sad anymore today."

"Okay." Maddy took Teresa's hand and led her into the bedroom.

Teresa pulled her shirt over her head and let it drop to the floor. Her bra followed a moment later. They stood just inches apart, undressing. When they were naked, Maddy led her to the bed, kissed her gently, and circled one hand around the back of her neck.

Teresa wrapped her arms around Maddy, pulling her closer. They fell into the bed, and Teresa felt Maddy's tongue slide over her. Teeth nipped at exposed flesh as she moved down Teresa's legs.

Teresa was drowning in the sensation, and for a moment felt a tendril of panic as if she would lose herself in all of this need. But then it was gone as passion turned it into something more powerful.

Maddy nuzzled her lips against the soft skin of Teresa's inner thigh, and Teresa's thoughts went fuzzy. Maddy worked her way up and down Teresa's body, claiming her. Filled with the intimate understanding that Teresa was hers to love, to care for, stand beside, and rely on, Maddy felt the powerful emotions settle deep in her heart.

When the last shudders of pleasure were gone, Maddy held Teresa close and kissed her again, a long, unhurried, and tender kiss that made Teresa want to cry.

"Thank you for being there today," she said. "I didn't get the chance to tell you that it felt good...inside...to know you were there." Her eyes welled up, and she pressed her fingers to them until she had her emotions under control. "Even if it didn't seem like it, it was important to me. I know it mattered to Brian."

They lay in the bed wrapped in each other's arms, and Maddy listened as Teresa recounted memories of David as a boy and then later when he was married to Fran. Teresa paused. "I should stop talking so much about them."

Maddy leaned in and kissed her. She pulled away and smiled slowly. "Don't stop. I want to hear about them."

Teresa drew back and studied Maddy's face in the soft glow of the lamp on the bedside table. Her heart had belonged to Maddy from the moment they had met. "I love you, Maddy."

Maddy laughed softly and pulled Teresa to her again. In those eyes, she saw love that was true and lasting. She felt it in her heart.

Chapter
Twenty-One

THE SETTING SUN was casting a brilliant display of vivid pinks and purples upon the underbelly of the cirrus clouds by the time Maddy and Brian got home. Maddy waited by the car as Teresa walked toward her over a growing carpet of oak and maple leaves.

Maddy took a pizza out of the car and set it on the Beetle's roof.

"Ah, you brought dinner." Teresa lifted the lid of the box and sniffed. "Mmm, pepperoni."

Maddy leaned in and affectionately cupped Teresa's face with her hand. "I figured you wouldn't mind."

"Not at all. I picked up some wine on my way home today."

"Good."

"You two were gone awhile," Teresa said, as Brian walked around the car and stood next to Maddy.

He rocked on his heels with his hands hidden behind his back. "We went shopping."

"Really?" Teresa glanced from Brian to Maddy curiously.

"Did you miss us?" Maddy said.

"Yeah, I was beginning to wonder what you two were up to. Were you able to get the paint colors you wanted?"

"All of them. I can't wait to see what the paint looks like on the walls."

"I got two rooms primed today, so we can start painting tomorrow."

"Aunt T, I got you a present." When he couldn't contain himself any longer, Brian pulled his hands out from behind his back and proudly held out a single, long stemmed red rose.

"Oh, Brian, it's beautiful." Teresa inhaled the delicate perfume. She hugged Brian to her and lifted him up in the air as she gave Maddy a smile.

"Let's go inside before the pizza gets cold." Maddy carried the pizza box and led the way to the apartment. Brian followed and charged up the stairs ahead of Teresa.

Before Maddy could set the pizza box down on the counter, Brian had dug into his coat pocket, pulled out a box, and shoved it into Teresa's hands as she reached the top of the stairs.

"Open it."

"Well," Maddy said, "I guess that's going to be an early Christmas gift."

"Should I wait?" Teresa stepped through the threshold and looked at Maddy.

"No. Go ahead and open it."

The hinges creaked slightly as Teresa opened the lid and pulled out a gold necklace with a silhouette of a woman holding a child.

"Brian, I love it."

"Come over here by the light, so you can see what's inscribed on the back," Maddy said and led Teresa by the arm.

Tears filled Teresa's eyes when she read the words: *To Momma T, Love, Brian.*

"Thank you," she whispered and pulled Brian into a fierce hug.

"Do you want to put it on?" he asked.

"Of course, I do." Teresa slipped the delicate chain around her neck and with Maddy's help hooked the clasp.

After a moment of quiet reverie, Maddy said, "All right you two, the pizza's going to get cold."

Teresa walked over and laid her hands on Maddy's shoulders. "The necklace is beautiful."

"Brian picked it out himself and decided what he wanted inscribed on the back."

"Can we eat? I'm starving," Brian said impatiently from behind them.

Teresa laughed and opened the pizza box. "Here you go." She pulled out two slices and set one on a paper plate for Brian and one for Maddy.

"Maddy, can you open the wine?"

"Sure. Milk for you, Brian." Maddy took two wine goblets out of the cabinets and filled them.

Teresa retrieved the milk from the refrigerator, poured it into a glass, and set it on the table in front of Brian.

"Sit and relax." Maddy pulled out a chair and pushed one out with her foot for Teresa.

They had been together a lot, mostly at Maddy's apartment working on finishing the house. Brian loved the old barn and spent hours exploring all the interesting places. He had fashioned a fort out of an old dropcloth in the hayloft and acted out fantastic stories of adventure on the weekends.

Teresa was leaving some of her things at Maddy's, little by little. They had an unspoken agreement that Teresa and Brian would come for dinner. They shared in the chores, Teresa painted, and Maddy continued to work with Brian on his schoolwork.

Their relationship had grown over the past several weeks, and Brian had shared with Maddy something he had been worried about asking Teresa.

"Do you want another slice of pizza, Brian?"

"Uh-uh. I'm finished. Can I be excused?"

"Sure. Put your plate in the garbage."

Brian cleared his plate from the table and then curled up on the couch to watch television.

Maddy leaned across the table and smiled warmly at Teresa. "He is such a good kid."

Teresa didn't say anything for a moment, and then she reached out and touched Maddy's hand. "He thinks the world of you."

"Last week he told me he didn't want to call you his aunt anymore."

"He saw the final adoption papers a couple of weeks ago and asked what he could call me."

"He told me about that, but I don't think that was the only reason." Maddy felt tears rising up in her eyes. "He blew me away when he told me."

"What did he say?" Teresa squeezed Maddy's hand gently.

"He told me that the day you two went to the cemetery and stood at the gravesite, he asked his mom if it was okay to call you momma. Brian said she told him yes because of your promise that you would take care of him."

"Oh, God, he said that?" It was Teresa's turn to feel tears burn her eyes.

"Momma T?" Brian's voice floated up from the couch.

"What Brian?"

"Do you think you'll have the house painted by Christmas?"

"By Christmas?" Maddy almost choked on her wine.

"I don't think so. That's a lot of painting," Teresa said. "Why?"

"I think a Christmas tree would look good in the front room downstairs. Don't you?"

"We'll have to see how much we get done." She looked at Maddy in stunned amazement. "Christmas, huh?"

"I had nothing to do with that, honest. He hatched that idea all by himself." Maddy poured herself some more wine.

"I could hire some college kids who are home on break. It's a crazy enough idea to just work. That is if you want to have a Christmas tree in the front room."

Maddy tilted her head and gazed at Teresa. "I...have this fantasy about the three of us spending Christmas morning in the house and having presents under the tree."

Teresa leaned forward and brushed a hand through Maddy's curls. She studied Maddy's profile, noting she wasn't looking at her. Teresa realized Maddy was embarrassed at having divulged her secret.

"How long have you had this idea?"

A half smile formed on Maddy's lips. "Since the Saturday you came over to help me with the barn door."

"You hardly knew me."

"I didn't have to. My heart already knew."

"Maddy," Teresa said with a smile in her voice. "I love you."

"I can't think of anything else I'd rather do than spend my life with you and Brian."

Chapter
Twenty-Two

THE TWO MONTHS leading up to Christmas were a whirlwind of activity. Amid the normal holiday bustle, Teresa and Maddy put in long hours painting. They decided early on to paint the downstairs and leave the upstairs, except for Brian's bedroom, unpainted until after New Year's Day.

It turned out to be a good decision because by the third week of December, the Christmas holiday was first in everyone's mind.

Teresa had hopes that this Christmas would be a happier time than the last two had been for Brian. Up until he was four, he had wakened on Christmas morning to find a stocking with his name on it filled with special treats, and a pile of gifts under the tree. Fran had meticulously wrapped his gifts and labeled them all from Santa Claus.

Fran's ability to cook a holiday meal with all the trimmings was an act of love in itself that only added to Teresa's bittersweet memories of the family's joyful celebrations.

She had tried to keep the tradition going, but it no longer felt like Christmas without Fran and David to share in it.

This year as Christmas drew closer, Teresa saw a glimmer of anticipation and excitement in Brian that had been all but lost over the past two years. For Maddy, it was the first Christmas in recent memory when her house had truly become a home again. There was nothing like a child to bring a completely new dimension to Christmas.

Teresa and Maddy couldn't help the giddiness they felt on Christmas morning when they heard Brian's thunderous charge out of his room. He stopped at the bottom of the steps and stared with wide-eyed wonder at the tree.

"Wow, I knew Santa would come last night!"

The tree was lit from top to bottom with skeins of white lights that Maddy and Teresa had meticulously wrapped in and around the branches earlier that week. The beautifully decorated tree dominated the corner of the living room as it reflected a soft white glow off all the ornaments and the gifts stacked beneath it.

"Brian, come over here. I want to show you something before we open presents." Teresa held her hand out to him, and together they walked to a small table Maddy had set up not too far from the Christmas tree.

"These candles are for your mom and dad. We thought it would be special to light them Christmas morning and keep them burning all day."

"So they can be with us." Brian reached out and touched each of the white candles with his hands.

Teresa nodded, and her voice cracked with emotion when she spoke. "By our remembering them, they share this day with us." Together, Teresa and Brian carefully lit each candle. One for her brother, Brian's father, David Parker, and one for her sister-in-law, Brian's mother, Frances Parker.

Brian stared at the flickering twin flames and then gave Teresa a warm, firm embrace. In that moment, Teresa felt the power of remembrance and knew that David and Fran would always be in their hearts.

They unwrapped presents one at a time and restacked them under the tree. Several times while Brian opened his, Teresa caught him glancing up at the two candles and staring at them for a moment or two.

Afterward, while he played with a magnetic building set, Teresa toasted bagels and made a pot of coffee. Maddy started measuring and chopping ingredients for their Christmas dinner feast and preheated the oven to roast the meat she had rubbed with a mixture of herbs, garlic, and olive oil the night before. Cooking in Maddy's family was an unhurried, relaxed affair. As a child, she had learned to cook in her mother's and grandmother's kitchens. It wasn't just about the mechanics of preparing the food. The camaraderie amid a lifetime of memories made the holiday rituals special over the years.

Brian came into the kitchen and climbed up on one of the stools to watch Maddy.

"Here, Brian." Teresa set the container of cream cheese and a plate with a bagel on it in front of him.

"Can I help, Maddy?"

"Eat your bagel, and then you can help me make the filling for the manicotti."

Teresa sat next to Brian, and he looked up at her, his gaze searching hers as though looking for an answer, and then unexpectedly he reached out and hugged her.

"I love you, Momma T."

"I love you, too, Brian."

"What time are Uncle Rich and Aunt Betty coming over?"

"They'll be here around noon."

Listening and smiling as they talked, Maddy cracked three eggs into a bowl that held a small amount of olive oil. She added flour to it, mixed everything together, and set it on the counter.

"Brian, I need your help now."

"Okay." He hopped off the stool and stood beside her.

She passed her hand over the ingredients gathered together on the counter. "All of this goes into this larger bowl."

"That's huge."

"It was my grandmother's. Are you ready?" She pried the lid off one of the plastic containers.

"Yeah." Brian upended the container, and a pound of ricotta cheese squished out into the bowl. He poured the grated mozzarella and Parmesan cheeses into the bowl while Maddy scraped in another pound of ricotta. She held out the spoon to Brian, and he licked the cheese off.

"Hey, don't I get a taste?" Teresa asked.

"Only the cooks get to taste it," Maddy said, with a mischievous gleam in her eye. "Brian, use this spoon to mix it." She handed him a clean one and held the bowl while he stirred everything together.

With the mixing done, Maddy shooed Brian away from the stove and heated a skillet. She poured some of the batter into the pan and watched the edges brown before flipping the crepe over with her fingers. When it was done, she set the crepe on a plate and repeated the process until all the batter was gone.

"Teresa, can you get me the sauce out of the refrigerator?"

"Sure." She retrieved the large plastic container that had been defrosting and opened it. She spooned a thin layer of sauce in the baking dish Maddy set on the counter.

Maddy filled each crepe with the cheese mixture and rolled it into a cylinder. Teresa set each one into the baking dish. They took their time, filling, rolling, and placing each crepe until the dish was full. Brian watched them from the table while he chewed on his bagel.

Teresa knew these moments they shared together were building new memories for Brian. Memories he would cherish as he grew older. Good times to balance the bad times, happy times to balance the sad ones. She wished there would be no more sad ones for him. There was no harm in praying for that.

Brian ran over and opened the refrigerator door for Maddy as she carried the baking dish across the kitchen.

"Thanks, Brian. Hey!" Maddy couldn't help but laugh when he stuck a finger in the sauce and licked it.

"Mmm, that tastes good."

"I'm glad you think so. Now go play."

Brian skipped out of the kitchen humming "Jingle Bells" to himself. Teresa walked over and hugged Maddy.

"Merry Christmas," they said to each other.

"Thank you for the candles," Teresa said. "I think it made him feel good about celebrating Christmas again."

"You're welcome." The doorbell rang and Maddy took Teresa's hand. "Come on, let's go greet our friends."

Brian was already at the door. "Hi, Uncle Rich. Where's Aunt Betty?"

"She's coming. Santa left a couple of gifts for you at our house."

Brian stuck his head out the door and would have run outside when he saw Betty had Teresa not held onto him.

"Brian, it's too cold to go out without a jacket. Step aside and let Uncle Rich in."

Rich scooped Brian up in his arms and gave him a hug before setting him back down. "See, I told you Santa would know where to find you."

"As if he wouldn't know." Teresa led Rich into the living room.

"Well, look at that tree. She's a beauty." Rich planted a kiss on Teresa's cheek and handed her two bottles of wine. "How about I get a fire going in that hearth?"

"That would be great."

He heard the throatiness in her voice and knew how bittersweet this day was. "You doing okay, T?"

"Yeah," she said at last. "It's tough but we're doing okay."

"Merry Christmas!" Betty walked through the front door carrying two bags filled with gifts. She set them down and surveyed the downstairs. "Teresa, this turned out fabulous."

"Thanks. Merry Christmas, Betty." Teresa gave her a hug, and Maddy followed with one of her own.

"What a lovely tree, and those candles are beautiful." Betty walked into the living room.

"Let me take your coats." Maddy carried them over to the closet and hung them up.

Brian was silent as he leaned against Teresa. "Tell Aunt Betty why we lit the candles," she said.

"They're for Mom and Dad."

Betty studied the two candles, and her eyes misted with tears. She held her arms out to Brian who ran in for a hug. "I think that's a wonderful way to remember your mom and dad on Christmas." She kissed his cheek soundly.

"Me, too." He stepped back and looked hopefully at the bags.

"Maybe we should see what Santa left for you at our house."

"Yeah!" Brian bounced on the balls of his feet as Betty handed him a package and sat on the couch to watch him open it.

Rich walked over and stood between Maddy and Teresa. He hooked his arms around their shoulders. "I'm amazed at what you two have accomplished in here."

"We make a good team."

"Yeah, we do." Teresa smiled when she met Maddy's gaze.

Rich tilted his head close to Teresa's ear and said, "I'm happy for you, T. I know David and Fran would be proud of you."

Teresa closed her eyes for just a moment and took a breath to steady her emotions. There were no guarantees in this life; of that, she was certain. There would be near perfect days like today and days when life's trials would challenge her and Maddy's love. Sometimes the best you could do was to face the world and take a chance…a leap of faith.

Teresa had learned an important lesson while surfacing through the layers of grief: Life and love were far too fragile to take for granted. She was lucky enough to be surrounded today by a loving family, one created by the threads of life that had come unraveled by tragedy and been mended together by a woman who dared to push past the darkness in Teresa's life. For the rest of her days, Teresa would remember how one promise had taken her on a life-altering journey that had opened the door to unparalleled joy when she allowed love back into her life.

FORTHCOMING YELOW ROSE TITLES

Family Affairs
by Vicki Stevenson

Assigned to work undercover in a small-town nursing home, insurance investigator Stacey Gardner sets out to find fraudulent medical claims. When she meets local resident Liz Schroeder, romance begins to bloom. But then she discovers widespread elder abuse of which the entire nursing home staff is aware, and she fears that the whole town may be participating in a cover up.

Liz persuades Stacey to trust her to accept help from her LGBT family in exposing the abuse. The family discovers an elaborate scheme that seems to defy exposure. Many of the nursing home staff members are dedicated to stopping Stacey at any cost, and the rest are too intimidated to reveal any information.

The family presses on, determined to bring justice to the perpetrators and relief to the suffering patients. While the bond of love between Stacey and Liz grows ever stronger, they face the agonizing reailty that success will spell the end of the chance at happiness that both women desperately crave.

Second Verse
by Jane Vollbrecht

Gail Larsen lives in the Tennessee woods and edits lesbian fiction for Outrageous Press. Good thing her professional life is satisfying, because she has not had much luck with her love life. Her first lover left her to pursue a different path; her next died in an accident. It has been two years since Gail has dated, and she is seeing a therapist, hoping to put her life back on track.

A special editing assignment throws Gail together with Connie Martin, one of the leading ladies of lesbian fiction. Gail is at first amused by Connie's Pit-bull personality in a Pekinese body, but amusement turns to attraction, and attraction to heart-wrenching anxiety that leaves Gail anguished and unsettled.

After an intense month working with Connie on her book, Gail's life-long friend Penny invites Gail back to Plainfield, Minnesota. Gail has always harbored an unanswered longing for Penny. Many old ghosts re-emerge, and they are forced to confront them. To Gail's annoyance and amazement, Connie tracks her down while she is in Plainfield, and now she fears she is trapped between two women, one she will never have and one she does not want. All she has ever wanted is a lifemate she could dance with for the rest of her life. Can she find someone who will last through the second verse?

Available January 2008

Family Values
by Vicki Stevenson

Devastated by the collapse of her long-term relationship, Alice Cruz decides to begin life anew. She moves to a small town, rents an apartment, and establishes a career in real estate. But when she tries to liquidate some of her investments for a down payment on a house, she discovers that she has been victimized by a con artist.

Local resident Tyler Sorensen has a track record of countless affairs without any emotional involvement. Known for her sexy good looks, easygoing kindness, and unique approach to problems, Tyler is asked by a mutual friend to figure out how Alice can recover her money.

While Tyler's elaborate plan progresses and members of her LGBT family work toward the solution, they discover that the con game involves more people and far higher stakes than they had imagined. As the family encounters unexpected obstacles, Tyler and Alice struggle with a growing emotional connection deeper than either woman has ever experienced.

ISBN 978-1-932300-89-5

The Heart's Strength
by Anna Furtado

In Book Two of the Briarcrest Chronicles Lydia and Catherine have become the caretakers of Briarcrest, and when a letter arrives from Catherine's old friend and former assistant, Sarah Pritchard, Catherine sets out on a journey that is both dangerous and embroiled in conflict.

When Catherine encounters an old friend in Willowglen, she forges a friendship with his daughter, Fiona, a tall, blue-eyed, raven-haired beauty. Fiona becomes an important ally when two churchmen from Spain set the town in turmoil claiming the authority of the Inquisition — with young Cate Pritchard at the center.

From their first meeting, Cate and Fiona are drawn to one another; however, Fiona refuses to act on her feelings out of loyalty and the oath she has given to Catherine. Cate, for her part, is uncertain about what to do with the new feelings she experiences for Fiona. And, one of the priest's has a deep, dark secret and an ulterior motive.

Finally, Lydia's arrival in Willowglen brings everything to a head and the women of Briarcrest, the Pritchards, and Fiona find themselves at the center of a terrible struggle — and each must dig deeply to find strength of heart amid the battle against the injustices they encounter. But will they all survive the ordeal?

ISBN 978-1-932300-93-2

OTHER YELLOW ROSE PUBLICATIONS

Sandra Barret	Lavender Secrets	978-1-932300-73-4
Georgia Beers	Thy Neighbor's Wife	1-932300-15-5
Georgia Beers	Turning the Page	978-1-932300-71-0
Carrie Brennan	Curve	1-932300-41-4
Carrie Carr	Destiny's Bridge	1-932300-11-2
Carrie Carr	Faith's Crossing	1-932300-12-0
Carrie Carr	Hope's Path	1-932300-40-6
Carrie Carr	Love's Journey	978-1-932300-65-9
Carrie Carr	Strength of the Heart	978-1-932300-81-9
Carrie Carr	The Way Things Should Be	978-1-932300-39-0
Carrie Carr	Something to Be Thankful For	1-932300-04-X
Carrie Carr	Diving Into the Turn	978-1-932300-54-3
Linda Crist	Borderline	978-1-932300-62-8
Jennifer Fulton	Passion Bay	1-932300-25-2
Jennifer Fulton	Saving Grace	1-932300-26-0
Jennifer Fulton	The Sacred Shore	1-932300-35-X
Jennifer Fulton	A Guarded Heart	1-932300-37-6
Anna Furtado	The Heart's Desire	1-932300-32-5
Anna Furtado	The Heart's Strength	978-1-932300-93-2
Lois Glenn	Scarlet E	978-1-932300-75-8
Melissa Good	Eye of the Storm	1-932300-13-9
Melissa Good	Red Sky At Morning	978-1-932300-80-2
Melissa Good	Thicker Than Water	1-932300-24-4
Melissa Good	Terrors of the High Seas	1-932300-45-7
Melissa Good	Tropical Storm	978-1-932300-60-4
Maya Indigal	Until Soon	1-932300-31-7
Lori L. Lake	Different Dress	1-932300-08-2
Lori L. Lake	Ricochet In Time	1-932300-17-1
K. E. Lane	And, Playing the Role of Herself	978-1-932300-72-7
J. Y Morgan	Learning To Trust	978-1-932300-59-8
J. Y. Morgan	Download	978-1-932300-88-8
A. K. Naten	Turning Tides	978-1-932300-47-5
Lynne Norris	One Promise	978-1-932300-92-5
Meghan O'Brien	Infinite Loop	1-932300-42-2
Paula Offutt	Butch Girls Can Fix Anything	978-1-932300-74-1
Sharon Smith	Into The Dark	1-932300-38-4
Surtees and Dunne	True Colours	978-1-932300-52-9
Surtees and Dunne	Many Roads to Travel	978-1-932300-55-0
Vicki Stevenson	Family Values	978-1-932300-89-5
Cate Swannell	Heart's Passage	1-932300-09-0
Cate Swannell	No Ocean Deep	1-932300-36-8

About the Author

Lynne Norris is the author of *Second Chances*. She lives in New Jersey with her partner and son.

VISIT US ONLINE AT

www.regalcrest.biz

At the Regal Crest Website You'll Find

- The latest news about forthcoming titles and new releases

- Our complete backlist of romance, mystery, thriller and adventure titles

- Information about your favorite authors

- Current bestsellers

Regal Crest titles are available from all progressive booksellers and online at StarCrossed Productions, (www.scp-inc.biz) and also at www.amazon.com, www.bamm.com, www.barnesandnoble.com, and many others.